A Dream Apart

As Dell Shannon:

CASE PENDING
THE ACE OF SPADES
EXTRA KILL
KNAVE OF HEARTS
DEATH OF A BUSYBODY
DOUBLE BLUFF
ROOT OF ALL EVIL
MARK OF MURDER
THE DEATH-BRINGERS
DEATH BY INCHES
COFFIN CORNER
WITH A VENGEANCE
CHANCE TO KILL

RAIN WITH VIOLENCE
KILL WITH KINDNESS
SCHOOLED TO KILL
CRIME ON THEIR HANDS
UNEXPECTED DEATH
WHIM TO KILL
THE RINGER
MURDER WITH LOVE
WITH INTENT TO KILL
NO HOLIDAY FOR CRIME
SPRING OF VIOLENCE
CRIME FILE
DEUCES WILD

As Elizabeth Linington:

THE PROUD MAN
THE LONG WATCH
MONSIEUR JANVIER
THE KINGBREAKER
ELIZABETH I (*Ency. Brit.*)
GREENMASK!
NO EVIL ANGEL

DATE WITH DEATH
SOMETHING WRONG
PRACTISE TO DECEIVE
CRIME BY CHANCE
PERCHANCE OF DEATH
POLICEMAN'S LOT

As Egan O'Neill:

THE ANGLOPHILE

As Lesley Egan:

A DREAM APART
THE BLIND SEARCH
SCENES OF CRIME
A CASE FOR APPEAL
THE BORROWED ALIBI
AGAINST THE EVIDENCE
RUN TO EVIL

MY NAME IS DEATH
DETECTIVE'S DUE
A SERIOUS INVESTIGATION
THE WINE OF VIOLENCE
IN THE DEATH OF A MAN
MALICIOUS MISCHIEF
PAPER CHASE

A Dream Apart

LESLEY EGAN

PUBLISHED FOR THE CRIME CLUB BY

DOUBLEDAY & COMPANY, INC.

GARDEN CITY, NEW YORK

1978

All of the characters in this book
are fictitious, and any resemblance
to actual persons, living or dead,
is purely coincidental.

Library of Congress Cataloging in Publication Data

Linington, Elizabeth.
A dream apart.

I. Title.
PZ4.L756Dr [PS3562.I515]   813'.5'4
ISBN: 0-385-13412-6
Library of Congress Catalog Card Number 77–82756

For Marge Bennett
in memory of Glendale

Life treads on life, and heart on heart;
We press too close in church and mart
To keep a dream or grave apart.

—*Robert Browning*

A VISION OF POETS

A Dream Apart

CHAPTER 1

It was like switching on a light. One second, blank dark; and then she was here, not knowing how or when or why. She shouldn't be here; she couldn't remember just where she'd been, what she'd been doing—only a moment ago?—in the house; she would remember in a moment. Nothing like this had ever happened to her before, and she was frightened. She felt her heart thudding. She was very tired, but that wasn't new; she was tired most of the time now.

She was standing just below the shallow crooked wooden steps to the narrow porch of the little house behind the church. It was very quiet: Sunday afternoon. It was still Sunday, wasn't it? No noise from the children in the apartment next door. A long way off, a motorcycle buzzed dimly.

Wesley had said those motorcyclists had been riding around the alley again; it was dangerous, he'd complained to the police.

Sunday. Again, after this awful week. What was she doing, standing here? She ought to be—she had been—in the house (as usual, as always) and then something had happened—

The light wasn't right. The sun was low in the sky, it was late afternoon. That couldn't be, because the last she remembered it wasn't late at all—church over, and lunch, and Wesley had left to go to the Thrift Store—

She turned to look at the sun, low toward the horizon—January, it would be dark by about six o'clock, but it couldn't be nearly six o'clock— There was a black-and-white police car at the curb, in front of the church.

Her heart thudded. She had always been afraid of policemen.

She didn't know where she'd been, what she'd done, since—she

grasped at definite memory futilely—she'd been where she was supposed to be, in the house. And what they'd say, what they'd ask—
must be going insane, things like this only happened to insane people—but she couldn't stand here, she had to go in. Where she was
supposed to be.

The old woman—having a fit, left alone, she'd never hear the last
of it—*insane*— Wesley, home? This late—

Sunday. Sunday? She still had on her best dress, she hadn't
changed after church. A prim, dowdy dress: the dress she'd been
married in; a while after she got it, she realized she'd never liked it.
She'd bought it two weeks after Mother Ruth's funeral, hadn't really
paid much attention to color or style or fit. She'd lost weight since,
and it hung on her loosely now, a sad dress, too pale a blue, with a
too-skimpy collar.

Couldn't just stand here. Must go in. Whatever they said or did.
The old woman—

She was frightened—*insane*—but she forced herself up on the
porch, opened the sagging screen door. The inner door was ajar; she
pushed it open and stepped into the little living room.

Into the Dream—the reality of the Dream.

All her life she had known it was waiting for her, somewhere
ahead. Now, without warning, it was here; and black terror engulfed
her.

The Dream had come to her ever since she could remember.
There would be months when it didn't come, and she'd forget all
about it; then it would come three, four, five times in succession.
The only person she'd ever told about it was Sharon, and Sharon was
dead now; nobody knew. It was queer that she'd never told Mother
Ruth. But even Sharon hadn't understood at all how the Dream so
terrified her.

"It's really nothing, is it?" she'd said blankly. "Nothing about it to
scare you so much, Eileen. Why should it?"

Perhaps telling about it, there wasn't. But even just telling it, she
felt the cold sweat break all over her. When it came, foggy and in-

complete and mysterious, it brought terror with it all too real, and
she would wake fighting the tangle of bedclothes, sweating, her heart
pounding and breath short.

In some of the places—before she was sent to Mother Ruth—
she'd been scolded and punished for having the Dream, making disturbance. Mother Ruth had just said, poor baby, no wonder you
have nightmares, never mind. But it was queer that Eileen had never
told her about it, that it was always the same one.

She didn't understand why it brought such terror, such abject guilt
and remorse.

It was always exactly the same.

She came from somewhere—outside or another room—into a
room. It wasn't clearly defined—foggy, subdued, indefinite. Darkish
walls, furniture around but not clearly seen; and—very clear, she always saw that—a sedate gray cat sat on the back of a chair. There
was the policeman, very tall and broad in a dark-blue uniform with
bright brass buttons, and there was someone else there too, but she
could never quite see who it was.

The policeman said something, but his voice was so muffled she
couldn't hear what he was saying, until a little while after she came
in it was clear and loud and he said, "It was deliberate murder."
Then more muttering, and all the while she knew he was talking
about something terrible—terrible and important to Eileen, because
whatever it was that had happened, it was all her fault, and the
awful consciousness of guilt was like a great heavy stone in her heart.
And then someone else said clearly, "I don't know why it had to
happen!" All the while the cat was washing its face, taking no notice at all. The policeman said, "We'll have to leave that to the detectives." And, "There's nothing you can do for her now." All the
while Eileen stood there frozen, silently screaming inside herself, "I
didn't mean to, I didn't mean to!"—but nobody paid any attention
to her. And when she woke each time from the terror, her cheeks
would be wet with tears of some awful loss and guilt.

Sometimes it came often, sometimes it didn't come for months.
But she had always known that it was a foreview of some reality to

come, that some day she would walk through a door and into the Dream, when it was really happening.

And now, at last, she had.

She saw and heard everything clearly. The policeman was tall and broad in his blue uniform. She'd never seen his face in the Dream; now she saw that it was square and snub-nosed, and he was young. It was a closed-looking face, wary and alert. He glanced sharply at her, and Wesley said, "Eileen!" It was Wesley, the other one in the room, except for the old woman in the wheelchair, its back toward the room, facing the little hall. She was quiet and still. She wouldn't be asleep, she would be furious, and Wesley would say feeble things—

"Eileen, where've you been? The most terrible—I don't understand—"

The policeman said, "Mrs. Endicott?"

Mrs. Endicott was the old woman. It always came as a little surprise to Eileen, even now, that she was Mrs. Endicott too. And just at that moment, irrelevant to anything else she was feeling, she thought it was strange that she'd never called her anything else. Like a stranger. What else could she have called her? *Mother* was Mother Ruth. *Mama*, just a word with dim connotation long ago: *nothing*.

Furious, she'd be furious—left alone so long (How long?)—she would—

She was immensely tired, numbly tired, but habit ingrained sent her toward the wheelchair, and she thought she started to say, "I'm sorry, Mrs. Endicott—"

"Just stay where you are, please, ma'am," said the policeman. *"There's nothing you can do for her now."*

"Eileen—Eileen—" said Wesley with a gasp. "I don't—where have you been? Why did you go out? Mother's dead. She's dead. The most terrible—"

"Dead," she said dully. It sounded stupid, but the panic fear, and heavy guilt, and the awful, reasonless remorse flooded all her being—because this was the reality, it was ten times worse than the Dream. Either she or Wesley said it again, over and over, *dead, dead.* She sat down carefully in the shabby green armchair. She said carefully, her heart in her throat, "She was all right—when—"

"*I don't know why it had to happen!*" said Wesley. "I don't know why! She was—she's been—you said—" he looked at the policeman wildly.

"*It was deliberate murder,*" said the policeman stolidly.

"Where were you?" asked Wesley. He sounded fretful and surprised. "She was never left alone—never. You never left her—"

Eileen was nearly suffocated with the rising panic; she held herself very still in the chair. She looked at Wesley sitting on one end of the couch. There was a pile of material beside him—the curtains, of course, the curtains he'd gone to buy at the Thrift Store, if there were any the right size; and she thought, of course he would have gotten the ugliest color there was. It was a dull saffron yellow, sleazy-looking stuff, like dull, cheap satin.

"You never left her!" he said. "I don't understand—all so terrible, so terrible—she's been—someone got in and—stabbed her—pair of scissors—I found her when— But where were you?"

She looked at him, feeling she'd never really seen him before. A thin little man going bald, with weak, pale-blue eyes behind his heavy glasses, making ineffectual flapping gestures. A silly little man. "Eileen?" He turned on the policeman then. "What are you doing? Aren't you going to do anything? I don't understand—just standing there—"

"Just take it easy, sir," said the policeman. He was writing in a notebook. "*We'll have to leave that to the detectives.*"

Eileen made herself stay motionless in the chair, but she felt her heart pounding so hard it might burst out of her body. And all the while the cat sat there—of course the old woman was dead, or she'd have been screaming about the cat—the fat gray cat who lived across the street but used to live here and sometimes came back. It had gotten in somehow, and it sat there on the back of the other chair calmly washing its face, until Wesley noticed it and jumped up in a flurry, shouting absurdly, "Shoo—shoo—get out of here!"

Affronted, the cat leaped down and stalked away toward the back of the house, stopping to rub its chin on the wheelchair. The chair and the old woman trembled a little, and Wesley said, "Oh my God —oh my God—" He collapsed onto the couch again.

Being real, the Dream went on, past what she knew. Steps on the porch, and another policeman, even taller, in uniform. They muttered together, across the room, their eyes on Eileen and Wesley; the other policeman went around in front of the wheelchair and looked. *Detectives. Murder.*

At least she'd always waked from the Dream, however terror-stricken, and forgot till the next time. Always knowing it waited somewhere ahead. And now it was real, it was happening, there was no waking up.

———◆———

It was toward the end of shift, and Varallo was alone in the detective office with their new plainclothes officer when the call came in. O'Connor was off somewhere with the Secret Service agents, though it was officially his day off; Katz and Poor were out on a burglary, and Forbes was home with the flu.

Sergeant Bill Dick on the desk relayed the call from the black-and-white, and Varallo took down the address. Putting down the phone, he said, "Overtime. New homicide." Their newest detective glanced across at him and stood up.

Changes had come again to the Glendale Police Department. Changes would always come, which didn't mean that anyone had to welcome them.

It was just after they'd cleaned up that sordid homicide of the three little kids, last June, that they'd lost Sergeant Fred Wayne. The end of a hot June Sunday, a quiet day for the force, no homicides, only a few heists to work; and Wayne had been downtown at LAPD headquarters watching a witness look at mug shots. He hadn't made any. Wayne had ferried him home, which was in La Crescenta, and been on his own way home back to Glendale, down La Crescenta Avenue, when a drunk juvenile in a stolen car broadsided him, doing about seventy, at the intersection of Roselawn. The juvenile was pried out of the wreckage with a broken ankle. Wayne was DOA at the emergency hospital.

Every cop on any force lived with the possibility of sudden

mayhem or death, a slightly more possible eventuality than the general run of the population knew; but it still had shock value when it came.

"And it's easy to say, worse if it was somebody else—worse!" O'Connor was saying that to Katz when Varallo landed at the hospital half an hour later. "At least he wasn't married—no family—so goddamn easy to say—but damn it, goddamn it, Joe, a slug from some punk's equalizer in the middle of a shootout, it's one thing—but damn it, at least it'd have been for a reason! That goddamned *nothing* of a teen-ager—and you know what a judge'll hand him—"

They hadn't had to guess about that; and there was no profit in swearing about it, though everybody did. It got written down as involuntary manslaughter: sixty days and three years' probation. There was all the grim fuss of an official funeral up at Forest Lawn, and then there was just the empty desk in the middle of the detective office.

It left a hole. In two ways, it left a big hole. They'd all worked with Wayne for years, and he'd been a good man to work with: always the same, easygoing, good-natured, efficient, tough when he had to be—a good cop. They missed him, big, hard-muscled Wayne lounging at his desk there. And it left a big hole another way, for in the past couple of years, with the transient population growing, street crime and other kinds of crime were way up, and they could have used two or three more plainclothesmen to help carry the load.

The official notices went out. A couple of the beat men were bucking for detective, but neither had the course credits built up to be eligible yet. There were just two applications sent in, and it was a while before they heard the results. In the middle of a busy Saturday afternoon, with Katz questioning a suspect in a homicide and Poor listening to three witnesses to a heist, Chief Jensen had come in with an official-looking letter in one hand and a rather peculiar expression on his face and marched over to O'Connor's desk. Two minutes later O'Connor had let out a bellow. "My sweet Jesus Christ!" Varallo and Forbes gave up trying to type reports and went to see what was happening. "They can't do this to us!" said O'Connor, outraged.

"Now, Charles," said Jensen, grinning, "be broad-minded. There really wasn't much choice—she was thirty points ahead of the other one on the exam. And these days, equal hiring practice—"

"A female detective, for God's sake! A fe—oh, God give me strength!" By that time of day, O'Connor always needed a shave; he had pulled his tie loose and taken off his jacket, and the worn shoulder holster holding the .357 magnum bounced as he flung himself back in the chair.

"Now," said Jensen, "she's been with LAPD for five years and has an absolutely clean record—been commended a few times. She sounds like a very competent girl, and you know we've said it'd be useful to have some female personnel—"

"Policewomen, yes—female detectives, I don't know," said O'Connor sourly.

"Don't be a male chauvinist, Charles," said Varallo with a grin. "She's certainly not inexperienced, coming from LAPD. What's her name?"

"Delia Riordan," said the chief, glancing at the papers in his hand. "Twenty-seven. I've got a very complimentary letter from an Inspector Danielson, praising her to the skies. Smart, reliable, cooperative, and so on and so on."

"Sounds fine to me." Jeff Forbes was intrigued and interested. "Maybe we could use a little womanly intuition around here."

O'Connor growled. He went on growling about it to Katharine when he got home, but Katharine was intrigued too. At the time, which was late October, she was looking very unlike his usual svelte, slim Katy, bulging amidships with the baby; and of course the first thing she said was, "I wonder if she's attractive or—twenty-seven. Well, the kind of girl who goes into it as a career—"

"There you are!" said O'Connor crossly. "If she is good-looking, every unmarried officer in the building in a tizzy, and all the wives jealous—"

"Don't be silly," said Katharine. Maisie, the outsize blue Afghan hound, sat up anxiously at O'Connor's tone and came over to plant a wet kiss on his cheek.

"—And," said O'Connor, getting out his handkerchief, "having to think twice before we use a cuss word—"

"Which will be very good training for all of you," said Katharine, "though you have quieted down some since I've been civilizing you, darling."

Varallo was cautiously positive toward the idea; when he told Laura, she was interested. "A lot of things that come along, a woman can be better with witnesses, some women would feel easier talking to another woman, and juveniles—most big forces have a good many policewomen these days, and LAPD tells us they can be invaluable. But it's not just so often you find one wanting to go on and make rank."

"She sounds interesting," said Laura. At the time she was bulging amidships too—she and Katharine had a bet on as to who would produce first. "I wonder if she's attractive, Vic."

"*Femminile eterno!*" said Varallo, amused. "What does it matter? If she's been an LAPD officer for five years, she'll know how to discourage unwanted admirers. Though I suppose if it created any rivalries in the office—Forbes and Rhys are still bachelors, and Dick Hunter—well, we'll have to take it as it comes." He wandered down the hall to inspect their best-ever baby, not quite a baby now but almost two, his darling Ginevra.

In due course Laura won the bet, riding decorously to the hospital in a cab while Varallo was downtown testifying at a burglary trial, and without much trouble producing John William just after midnight.

"Exactly what we wanted," she said to Varallo at 1 A.M., sounding pleased with herself. "Except that you won't let me give him a really interesting name. If it'd been another girl I could have called her Francesca—"

"After some of the wild ideas you came out with, no way!" said Varallo. "It's bad enough that I'm stuck with Lodovico, I wouldn't wish it on a dog—John is quite good enough."

"At least he's got your hair," said Laura in satisfaction, beaming down at the new arrival's soft gold fuzz. "And Katharine owes me lunch at Pike's Verdugo Oaks as soon as we can both make it. You did call them, didn't you?"

Varallo grinned down at her. "Well, you only won the bet by half a length, *cara*. When I got Charles he was gibbering—Katharine's just started, and they were leaving for the hospital. I'd better go over and lend him some moral support."

But there was a list of cases to work, and he had to get a little sleep. O'Connor never showed up all next day; Varallo had just gotten home and was relaxing over a brandy and soda before going to the hospital to see Laura when O'Connor called. He sounded exhausted. He said, "Never again. Never again will I go through all this. My God, how does anybody stand it four or five times? My God, I was never so scared—my God, I'm glad that's over with, and never again—"

"Don't babble, Charles. Katharine all right? And—"

"They said so. I guess so," said O'Connor doubtfully. "Oh, it's a boy."

And he didn't want a junior any more than Varallo; grudgingly he'd agreed to Vincent Charles.

Their new detective had come to them in late November, not quite two months ago. The chief had ushered her in one Monday morning, evidently feeling she needed a special sendoff.

Out of the corner of his eye Varallo noticed Forbes gallantly concealing disappointment; if the new detective was as smart as her record said, he hoped she didn't notice it too. But nobody would have known if she had.

You certainly couldn't call her a glamor girl, he thought; plain Jane all right, Miss Delia Riordan. Poker face, and all business. But she had a nice, warm contralto voice and a friendly little smile as she said serenely she hoped they'd find her satisfactory.

Katz was the first one to go out on a call with her—a heist; and he said she was efficient, all right. Very good with the witnesses, and offered to type the report, and it was clean and competent. She was a better typist than anyone else in the office, but O'Connor said that was only natural—it seemed to come easier to women.

She settled down quietly and easily, friendly with all of them, never putting herself forward. It looked strange at first to see her there at Wayne's old desk, but they were getting used to it. In time to come, probably she'd be accepted as just another detective, a helpful partner to have on a case, only secondarily recognized as female.

She must have been there six weeks before Varallo, slouched in his desk chair mulling over a statement, one afternoon last week, found himself staring at her absently and realized with faint surprise that there really wasn't anything wrong with their plain Jane's looks.

She was sitting upright typing briskly, intent on the job. It was, he thought, the overall effect she gave, at first glance, of utter plainness; not going out of the way to call attention to herself. A medium-sized, nondescript sort of girl, rather dowdy, you thought. But looked at twice, her features weren't bad at all: roundish face; nice peaches-and-cream complexion; small, straight nose; a rather large, firm mouth; blue eyes; eyebrows almost straight; ordinary dark-brown hair in a neat short cut, only curled a little around her face. Not much makeup, discreet lipstick, colorless nail polish. And she always wore plain dark pantsuits or plain dark dresses a modest length to the knee, with low-heeled shoes. Tiny gold hoop earrings in pierced ears, a plain gold ring with a dark stone on one hand. No glamor girl, Delia; but she wouldn't be at all unattractive, fixed up a little. Varallo wondered if she ever did fix herself up, eye shadow and mascara and a slinky evening dress—was there a boyfriend? Somehow he felt doubtful. Single-minded, that was Delia; really set on being a career cop. Which was unusual. But there were some; and some of them were damned good.

At least she wasn't going to cause any disruption in the office. For any reason.

He mentioned his discovery to O'Connor as they walked across the parking lot that afternoon. "You look at her three times, Charles, she's not at all bad-looking."

"You look at her three times," said O'Connor querulously, rattling his keys in his hand. "I'm just thankful she isn't making eyes at everything in pants. Only these days that's the wrong way to put it; most women seem to live in pants too." He yawned hugely. "How do people live through this? Why does anybody want to? I haven't had any sleep in three nights." He looked at Varallo bitterly. "First you can't get to sleep for expecting it, and then—"

"He's still yelling all night? Some of them will."

"Built-in alarm," said O'Connor through another yawn. "Two A.M. on the dot, he sounds off. Straight through till six. Katy can sleep days, for God's sake. And, for God's sake, the last week it's got

Maisie all upset. Soon as the baby starts in, so does she—howling like a banshee. It's a wonder the neighbors haven't called in a complaint."

Varallo burst out laughing. "Give them time. You just don't live right, or maybe we've been lucky. Johnny's just the way Ginevra was —settles down as good as gold and not a peep out of him all night."

O'Connor growled wordlessly and climbed into the Ford. Slamming the door, he glared out balefully and said, "All I say is—never again! I'd never live through it all again."

"They outgrow it eventually, *amico.*"

"And eventually I could be dead from lack of sleep." O'Connor backed out of the slot violently and turned out of the lot. Getting into the Gremlin, Varallo saw their lady detective emerge from the building and head for her car. That was another rather interesting thing about her: she drove an ancient silver-gray Mercedes, not the kind of car many career cops could afford to buy. Of course, she'd have gotten it fourth- or fifth-hand; when it was brand new she'd have been about seven years old.

At the moment, things were for once a little slow. There was a bunch of counterfeiters running around town, and the Secret Service agents in and out as a consequence, and the continued vandalisms, and the usual heists with a couple of APB's out. Last night had been quiet for Saturday; Hunter and Rhys on night watch had had the usual drunks, an assault, a hit-and-run. Everybody else was out on something at five-twenty when Patrolman Tracy called in a homicide. Varallo put down the phone and looked across at Delia Riordan.

"Overtime," he said. "New homicide. We'd better go out on it and start the ball rolling at least."

She stood up at once. "Well, it's been a slow day. What's it sound like?"

"Offbeat," said Varallo. He rang the lab and told Burt and Thomsen to meet them there. They took the Gremlin; as he made the light at Brand and Wilson he cast one glance down Brand, which was looking rather dilapidated these days, with the big Webbs' department store gutted to a shell by fire, and a few other stores empty and closed. Delia was silent beside him.

It was south down on Central; it turned out to be a corner where one of the narrow side streets, Elm, ended abruptly at the wider main street. There were two black-and-whites in front. But the address wasn't a house; it was a church, a small, square, plain church, an old frame building painted white and needing new paint. There was a plain signboard over the door, stark black letters: *Word of God Pentecostal Mission Church*. A small, square notice board hung neatly beside the door; Varallo's long sight made it out easily. *Sunday school 9 A.M. Sunday worship service 11 A.M. Come and worship. All welcome.*

They got out of the car. Tracy was waiting for them beside one of the patrol cars. He came forward. "What have we got?" asked Varallo.

"Murder One, looks like. Something funny, you ask me." Tracy talked directly to him, not so much ignoring Delia as bypassing her; the uniformed men weren't used to her yet. "I got chased down here about half an hour ago. When I got here and saw what it was, I called a backup—preserve the scene for you. Fenner's inside keeping an eye on. It's the house behind the church here—I guess it's all one property, the minister of the church gets the house to live in, see? Not much of a church, I guess—not much of a house." He shrugged. "Anyway, it was the minister called in. I haven't made much sense out of him. Rev. Mr. Endicott—Wesley Endicott. You'll probably read him the way I do—he kind of reminds me of the White Rabbit in *Alice*. He says he came home and found his mother dead. She was an invalid of some sort—in a wheelchair. That's about all he says except that his wife should have been there. And just before Fenner got here, the wife turned up."

"You said Murder One?" said Delia.

"She's been stabbed with a pair of scissors," said Tracy laconically. "All he says is, how could it happen, Eileen was here. Eileen's the wife."

"What about her?" asked Varallo.

"A zombie," said Tracy. "She walks in, and he jitters at her,

where've you been, she just sits down and says nothing, looking like
death warmed over."

"Well," said Varallo, "the lab boys'll be here, and the doctor.
Then you can get back on tour. Thanks."

A narrow cement walk led around the side of the little church. A
scant fifteen feet separated the rear of the church building from a
small, nearly ramshackle frame house right at the rear of the lot. It
backed up to the asphalt drive of a small apartment building front-
ing on the side street, no fence between. There were three shallow,
crooked steps to a mean little porch, a sagging screen door, an inner
door standing open. A single garage was at the left side, where a narrow drive led out to the street.

Varallo pushed the screen door open with one foot. He'd been a
cop for sixteen years, twelve on the force upstate and then starting in
again here; it was automatic to think about latent prints. And it was
a pity, of course, about the seniority, but that couldn't be helped,
and it was his own fault, resigning as captain up there. The hole in
the office had left an opening for sergeant, but Katz had the seniority on this force, and that was all right; Joe was a good cop and had
earned the rank.

They went into a very small, shabby living room. Dirty beige
walls were long in need of paint. There was a drab thin rug, of inde-
terminate color; an old couch upholstered in faded beige tapestry;
and a couple of old chairs, green, brown. No TV. A fake mantel
with a narrow aperture below, with a small electric heater there. It
was on, glowing fierce red. This winter had been exceptionally cold,
with a good deal of rain early, and then none at all; but today had
been warmer, and the heater made the room hot and stuffy.

Fenner was standing beside a wheelchair, which was facing into a
little hallway out of the living room. A man was sitting on the
couch, a woman in the green chair opposite. The two detectives
went to look at the corpse, and Fenner stepped aside.

It wasn't a very pretty corpse; corpses seldom are pretty. The body
sagging in the wheelchair was an old woman, not fat or thin but
subtly misshapen; they noticed the swollen knuckles on the hands
across the plump little stomach, the twisted, swollen feet where old
felt slippers had taken on the distorted shape. Her head lolled down;

they could see only part of her lined, gray face, one eye half open in a grotesque wink. They could see the handles of the scissors, where the blades had been thrust together into her chest.

Varallo said, "It took some strength—" And Delia reached out and put one hand under the dead woman's chin, and lifted her head. "Hey," said Varallo, "the doctor—"

"I just wanted to see her face." But it wasn't easy to guess what she might have looked like in life. Wrinkled gray skin, thin face, no makeup, scanty gray eyebrows, long gray hair in a neat knot on top of her head. Delia let the head down again as Varallo contemplated the wheelchair and the carpet around it. Never any telling where the lab boys would pick up useful evidence.

"What are you doing?" asked the man. He looked at them wildly. He was a young man, probably younger than he looked: thin, blondish, balding, with a narrow chin and protuberant china-blue eyes behind rimless glasses.

Delia was looking at the girl, who sat rigid and motionless in the chair. She was thin and small and colorless. She had a good deal of light brown hair, untidy on her shoulders. She was wearing an unbecoming light-blue dress, a white cardigan, beige cotton stockings, and shabby black pumps.

Varallo glanced at Delia, and just as with any pair of detectives, the message passed: You take her, I'll take him.

The lab truck pulled up outside, and Dr. Goulding's car behind it. Varallo touched Endicott's arm. "We'll be in the way here, sir. I'd like to talk to you. Can we just step outside—or maybe into the church?"

Endicott peered up dazedly. "Oh yes. Yes, of course—the church." He stumbled to his feet. Varallo followed him out, leaving the girl to Delia.

CHAPTER 2

The lab men were unpacking their equipment, the doctor bending over the corpse. This was just a new job, a new problem—but not, of course, to the Endicotts. Delia took the girl out of the house, but it was now full dark and cold; lacking any other place, she put her into the back seat of Dr. Goulding's plush new Chrysler, got into the front seat, and twisted around to face her, switching on the roof light. She got out her notebook unobtrusively. "Mrs. Endicott, we're sorry to have to bother you at a time like this," she said gently. "I know you're shocked and upset, but if you could answer a few questions—"

"I'm all right," said the girl in a thin voice. She didn't look it. She could be, Delia thought, quite a pretty girl. The brown hair was thick and slightly wavy, and she had very large blue eyes, a delicately molded mouth. But she was much too thin, and she looked very tired, very frightened; her voice was thready and curiously indifferent.

"You were out this afternoon? You didn't get home until your husband had come in and found his mother dead?"

"The policeman was there when I came."

"Your mother-in-law was an invalid? Confined to a wheelchair?"

"Oh yes. It's arthritis," said the girl. "I have to do everything for her. Take her to the bathroom, give her her bath, get her into bed and out. She can move the chair around herself, a little. It got a lot worse suddenly, you see. The doctor said sometimes it does. Rheumatoid arthritis. When we were first—when we came here, she was getting around just like anybody, only lame and stiff sometimes."

"When was that?" asked Delia, giving her time.

She waited a moment, as if to think. "Nearly three years ago.

When they gave Wesley this church. It got a lot worse suddenly, so she had to have the wheelchair, and I have to do everything for her."

"I see," said Delia. "Then you couldn't leave her alone very long, or very often?"

"No," said the girl. "No." She was too pale already, but suddenly she went green-white and shut her eyes and sagged sideways. Delia whipped open the front door, got into the back seat, and briskly shoved the girl's head down between her knees.

"Just take a few deep breaths. Better in a minute. Do you feel sick?"

"I'm all right. I'm sorry." She sat up shakily. "Thank you, I'll be all right."

Delia gave her a minute. "You understand, we want to get to work on this right away. And you can't go back to the house for a while; the lab men are busy there. They'll want to take your fingerprints, and your husband's."

"What for?"

"Comparison. There'll be a good many of yours everywhere, and if they find any others they'll have to sort them out. Are you feeling better now? You couldn't leave her alone much, but today you did. For how long? Where were you?"

"I'm not sure—how long," said the girl faintly. "No, I shouldn't have—I—it was hot in the house. She's always cold—wants the heater turned up, and it was hot and stuffy, I—had to have some fresh air. I went out—just for a walk."

"What time was that?"

"I don't know. I haven't got a watch—I mean, my watch stopped running and I haven't been wearing it. About two o'clock, I guess."

"Where did you go?"

"I went—up to that shopping center. Just to look in windows."

"The Galleria. Did you walk all the way up there?"

"Yes. Yes, I—and then I suddenly realized how long I'd been gone, it was getting late, and I—came home."

"Did you lock the door when you left?"

"No, I—it's never locked, except at night." She looked surprised.

"We'd like you and your husband to look around, see if anything is missing from the house."

"Missing. Why? You think—a burglar—came in and— There isn't anything to steal," said the girl simply. "The church board doesn't pay Wesley much. We get the house, but nearly everything in it needs fixing. I don't have any jewelry, neither did she—there wasn't any money there."

"Well, we'd like you to look, please."

"There wasn't anything. It must have been so terrible for Wesley to find her—like that," the girl said suddenly. "I'm so sorry about it." Her eyes shut again; she leaned against the seat looking ready to die.

Delia regarded her, curious and concerned. A state of shock she knew; this was something else. She wondered what Varallo was getting from the minister. Minister: he didn't exactly look the part. Well, you didn't always get coherent answers from people who'd just stumbled across a corpse. Tomorrow, hopefully, getting the formal statements, more might emerge to the point.

She left the girl there and went back to the house to see what the doctor and lab men had to say.

———◆———

Varallo had heard a good deal from Endicott, and maybe some of it was important, more likely not. Shock had set Endicott babbling. He dropped his keys twice on the path to the back door of the church, and fumbled nearsightedly at the lock. "The furnace is off—but it isn't working properly anyway—there've been a few complaints, it's been so cold, I really didn't like to write to the board—after all the other—I don't know where you'd like to—"

It was an ugly, bare little church, with stained pine pews to accommodate no more than fifty or so. Bare wooden floor, a tiny altar only a few steps up from the body of the church. Ancient venetian blinds covered the narrow windows. At either side of the altar hung a scriptural text stenciled in uncompromising black on a white-painted board nailed to the wall. The one on the left warned THOU GOD SEEST ME, the one on the right, THIS NIGHT SHALL THY SOUL BE REQUIRED. It was very cold in the church.

Varallo got him to sit in one of the front pews. "If you can just answer a few questions, Mr. Endicott. What time did you leave the house?"

"I think about one o'clock—I'm not sure." The narrow, pale face was pinched, distressed; he put a hand to his glasses nervously. "The service was over at noon—I always try to be prompt, people don't—don't seem to like very long sermons—once or twice something was said—and everyone—everyone left nearly at once." He swallowed; the distress in his eyes deepened. "I'm so afraid—terrible—it's caused trouble, and all the talk—not done the church any good, it's been very worrying—and on top of everything else, the job, I've been so afraid I'd lose—I beg your pardon."

"I asked, where did you go?"

"That Thrift Shop on Colorado Boulevard. The curtains in the living room—falling to pieces, Eileen said, and there might be some we could use—I—I should explain," said Endicott with painful dignity, "ours is a very small sect—but growing, we must trust growing all the time—I've tried my best, I know I haven't fulfilled the expectations of our board of deacons, I've tried, but people are difficult to reach—so much materialism and sin all around—what I mean to say, we're not a wealthy church, the board can only pay its pastors a very nominal salary, we're expected to—to look after ourselves and consider our calling as a labor of Christian love. I have a—a regular job —at the parking lot on Maryland and Broadway—" He kept adjusting the old-fashioned rimless glasses in a habitual nervous gesture. "You see, it was Mother's dearest wish that I be ordained—her father was one of the founders of our church—and she paid my expenses while I was at divinity school, but after that—when the deacons gave me the church here, when old Rev. Hoby passed away, she said—she said it was only right—I should stand on my own feet. And of course—"

"Mr. Endicott." With difficulty Varallo got a word in. "You left here about one o'clock? Your mother and your wife were here then?"

"Oh yes, certainly. I didn't want any lunch—Eileen was fixing something for Mother. I had to wait for a bus—what? No, I don't have a car. We've never had—I couldn't afford—of course, that was why—" he swallowed and got himself back on a more coherent course. "It all took some time, there were measurements, I'd forgotten the tape measure, but they had a yardstick—it would have been better for Eileen to do it, women know more about these things, but of course she couldn't leave Mother—" Suddenly Endicott put both hands to his face.

"You came home about five o'clock, a little before. Did you call the police as soon as you discovered her?"

"I think so. Yes. I was—so surprised—Eileen not there. I thought —I thought Mother was asleep—and then—" Endicott rocked a little back and forth.

Varallo thought he wouldn't get much more from him now. Get formal statements tomorrow. He explained, apologized, about the lab men working in the house. "They won't disturb anything more than they can help. We'd like you to have a look and see if anything's missing."

"Missing?"

"Stolen," said Varallo patiently.

"Oh. Oh, do you think—a burglar broke in and—oh, I didn't think of that," said Endicott. "I hadn't thought about—about who —it was just so terrible, seeing her like that—I never—" And then he straightened and uttered a kind of strangled sob; his eyes were suddenly wild. "Her check! Mother's check! It came yesterday—it's the only money in the house—the only thing to steal! If it's gone—"

"All right, we'll have a look. A check for how much? Do you know where it was?"

"Six hundred dollars. She put it in her pocketbook, the way she always—if it's been stolen—she never would give it to me till I was ready to start for the bank—"

Varallo left him gibbering and went back to the house.

———◆———

"I'll tell you one thing right off the bat," Burt was saying to Delia as Varallo came into the living room. "We'll never get anything off the scissors." He hadn't attempted to remove them from the body; leave that for the doctor. "When you pick up a pair of scissors to use how they're meant to use, sure, you'll leave partial prints here and there. Use 'em like that"—he nodded at the body—"blades shut, like a dagger, you've got your hand wrapped around the handles to get a grip. No prints."

"No, I see," said Delia.

"In fact, it's funny," said Burt, "seeing how much time we spend looking for prints, how very seldom it is we get a print good enough to clinch a case. I don't think we will here, either." But he'd been looking; various surfaces all over the room had been dusted, and all the metal parts of the wheelchair. Thomsen had evidently taken all the photos he wanted and left the Speed Graphic on the little mantel. Dr. Goulding straightened up from the body and snapped his bag shut.

"I can't tell you much until I've had a better look," he said shortly. "The morgue wagon's on the way."

"Any time estimate?"

"You know better, Vic. Wait for it. That damned electric heater —it must be eighty-five in here. Maybe confuse the time of death some. Let me have a look inside and I'll make a guess."

"Would you like to make another?" asked Delia. "Did it take much strength, Doctor? Could a woman have done it?" Varallo looked at her.

Goulding looked curious. "I wouldn't have said so, but you can't be dogmatic about a thing like that. She wasn't a big woman, no great amount of fat to get through, and given some strong motive— You have somebody in mind?" Goulding was police surgeon by courtesy on his own time, having ample means and a lifelong fascination with detection; he claimed the two professions had a lot in common.

"I don't know—not really," said Delia.

"Well, I'll open her up and give you something more definite tomorrow," said Goulding briskly, and took himself off.

"I should have warned him about Eileen in the back seat," said Delia, absently.

"So what about Eileen? Endicott keeps saying she never left the mother alone. Why did she?" He heard Delia's succinct report on that and said, "Well, it's possible. Even probable. She must have had a fairly boring time, stuck here with an invalid all day. Though they must have friends—some of the good Christian churchgoers to come and sit with the pastor's mother, help look after her out of charity. You would think."

"You don't buy the Christian charity?"

"Let's say it isn't as common as it should be. What about the girl?"

"I don't know," said Delia. "She's a funny one. She acts scared of something. But it could be just—well, we see homicides. The average citizen doesn't. I suppose she could be just frightened and upset, seeing the body."

Varallo agreed. "Have a look around for the old woman's handbag. Endicott says there should be a check in it."

"Two handbags," said Burt from the floor, where he was dusting the underside of the metal armrest of the wheelchair. "One in the closet off the front bedroom, one on the bed in the back bedroom."

"I should think that'd be it." Varallo edged past him into the hall. A small square kitchen was at the left, a tiny bathroom between that and a small bedroom. Thomsen was looking around in there. It was barely furnished: a rag rug on the floor, a single bed with a faded blue chenille spread, white cafe curtains on a double tier of dingy brass rods at the one window, a meager wardrobe built into one wall. Everything seemed clean enough, just poor and cheap and old. There was a worn black leather handbag in the middle of the bed. It had been dusted: Varallo picked it up and opened it.

"Well, *guardare*," he said. "There it is, and very nice too." He held it up: a light-green check, elegantly imprinted. "Commonwealth Security Funds, Incorporated. To the order of Mrs. Rhoda Endicott, six hundred and no-tenths dollars."

Thomsen wandered over to look. "That'll be one of those mutualfunds outfits," he said interestedly. "A lot of older people with any capital go in for it. You can set up a monthly payment out of the interest."

"Yes," said Varallo thoughtfully, "and can we have a rough guess as to what size the capital might be, to produce six hundred bucks a month? It'd have to be at least in the neighborhood of a hundred grand, wouldn't it? Poor as church mice, indeed. She could afford to pay Wesley's way through divinity school—I think she really might have bought them some new curtains too, instead of chasing Wesley down to the Thrift Shop."

"Curtains?" said Delia. He explained economically, and turned the check over. It wasn't endorsed.

"Not until Wesley started off to the bank. And then again it is possible to give the punks credit for too many brains. In spite of experience, we all do it. Some of the casual burglars mightn't know what a check is. Or, conversely, be smart enough to leave it lay, not invite trouble trying to cash it. The bag wasn't open?"

"Just sitting there on the bed," said Thomsen.

"Yes. And whether anything's missing or not, it could still have been the casual burglar," said Varallo. "In fact, probably. Picking a place at random, finding the door unlocked and then panicking when he found the old lady home. My God, it's seven-thirty. They'll probably send the night watch out—ask around if the neighbors saw anything—sometimes we get a break." He was starving, he realized suddenly; he hoped Sergeant Harrison had called Laura to tell her he'd be late. Delia had disappeared; he went looking and found her in the front bedroom off the living room. The morgue attendants were just coming in with a stretcher.

The front bedroom wasn't much bigger than the other, just enough to accommodate twin beds, not much else but a pair of three-drawer chests. There was a narrow walk-in closet. Delia was contemplating one of the beds. "Come on, let's knock off," said Varallo. "Tomorrow's another day. What's that?"

"More curtains," said Delia. "I should think, for this window." The material outspread on the bed was green cotton twill, stretched nearly the length of the bed. A yardstick lay along it, a little crooked, and a cut had been started about a yard and a half down.

Varallo yawned. "Come on," he said. Having seen a lot of homicides, he would take a bet that this one would end up in Pending; no leads. Ten to one, the casual breaker-inner. There were just a couple of reservations in his mind on it, thinking about Wesley and that check—the curtains—and Eileen, of course.

He drove Delia back to headquarters for her car, and headed for the house on Hillcroft Road up in Rossmoyne. Laura had the driveway lights on for him. As he came up to the back door, he detoured to inspect Alida Lovett climbing up the trellis. Thank God for this colder winter, no aphids, and with business slow at the first of the month, he'd gotten all the roses pruned back on time. It had fallen to freezing one night, but they didn't seem to have taken any harm; if it went down again he'd start to worry, but sufficient was the evil. He went in to an appetizing smell and found Laura at the stove.

"Yes, of course they called. Business picking up again, I take it." She was back to size fourteen again, her bright brown hair neat and shining, her eyes smiling at him. "Anything interesting?"

"It seldom is," said Varallo. "Probably a very ordinary homicide. Though—well, leave it till tomorrow. How are the offspring?"

"You've got three minutes to go see while I broil your hamburger."

He went down to look into the nursery. The offspring were both sound asleep, healthy and peaceful. And Gideon Algernon Cadwallader, that plump gray-and-white feline, was gravely playing watchcat on top of the dresser. He gave Varallo a regal green glance.

Bob Rhys and Dick Hunter, on night watch, went out on the homicide and were briefed by Burt and Thomsen, still poking around in the house. The body was gone. "I guess the minister and his wife are in the church," said Burt. "Varallo said you might talk to the neighbors—maybe somebody noticed something."

"What a hope," said Hunter.

"Well, we can ask," said Rhys. "You pick up anything?"

"I don't know. Have to sort out all the latents. We'll be finished here in half an hour."

You couldn't say there were many neighbors to the little house behind the church on the corner. Next to the church, on Central, was an old rambling California bungalow; next to that, a small-appliance store, with its own parking lot in front. The small apartment directly behind the house, and across the street on Elm two or three houses might have a view of the Endicott place. Rhys tried the big bungalow first; he couldn't see any lights, and didn't get any answer to the bell, but there was a sign of some kind in the front win-

dow, so he got out his flashlight. FOR LEASE, said the sign, and
Rhys was annoyed. Silly place to put it: Probably they weren't too
anxious to lease it—somebody's tax writeoff. He met Hunter on the
first floor of the apartment. It was only a six-unit place, and the two
tenants Hunter had talked to hadn't anything to tell them.

At the upper rear left, they heard something from Mr. Peter
Riggs, interrupted over a can of beer and the sports page. "What
d'you wanna know for? You're *cops*? You don't mean it—a *murder*?
Who? Well, I'll be goddamned! I will be— Hey, Betty! Betty, you'll
never guess what—that old biddy's got herself murdered!"

"Do you know the Endicotts?" asked Rhys.

"Knew her all right. From last summer, right after we moved here.
You never heard such a fuss."

"Oh, did we know her," said his wife. They looked like ordinary
run-of-the-mill honest citizens. "Always complaining about the kids.
There are only four kids here, our two and the Spracketts', but look,
you know kids. They get careless—they forget. The school's up on
Glendale Avenue, they come home down Central, and it's easier for
them to cut through the church grounds and come in the back way.
The old lady kicked up a fuss about that, trespassing, always complaining to Mr. Burns, he's the manager. Then, they got to play
somewhere, and you can see how close that house is to the driveway
here; well, that's not our fault. Complaints about the noise they
made—well, I ask you. At least, since the weather got cold, I suppose
she had the windows shut, we hadn't heard any more out of her. Did
you say she's been *murdered*? Well, I never. Who by?"

"We don't know yet," said Rhys. "Did either of you see anybody
going in there this afternoon?"

They both shrugged. "Who was looking?" said Riggs. "I been
watching the game on TV, and Betty's been fooling around the
kitchen all day."

At the three houses across the street they drew a near blank too.
The Hennickers, an elderly couple, had been napping all afternoon,
hadn't seen anything; Mrs. Eddy in the middle house hadn't been
home. Mr. Trilling, deaf and palsied, had something to say when
they'd bellowed at him loud enough.

"Yes, sir, I did see somebody going near that house today. You never do except of a Sunday, acourse. But this was after all the church crowd left, couple of hours, anyway. I wouldn't have noticed, I was waiting for a movie to start on the TV, sort of just looking out the window, not thinking of anything. Why you want to know? There been a burglary or something?"

"Could you describe the person you saw?" asked Hunter. "You were alone here?"

"That's right, my daughter lives here with me, but she was out somewheres. It was just a kid—a boy, I guess—kind of hard to tell nowadays," and he cackled. "They all look alike."

"Did you see him actually going up to the house?" asked Rhys.

"Well, no, but he was walking along the sidewalk just about where that cement walk goes in."

"Thanks very much," said Hunter. Nothing.

"Well, he was!" said Trilling, divining their rejection. "I may be deaf as a post, but my eyes are still working pretty good!"

"Yes, sir. Thanks."

They went back to the office and found a new heist job waiting.

———◆———

Once she had wished so bitterly, with all the passion in her, that she had died with the rest of them in the accident. She ought to have died with them. Half an hour later she would have been with them, and then all the rest of this misery and fear and trouble would never have happened.

People had said, the grace of God you weren't with them. If there was such a thing as the grace of God, she would have been.

All the rest of this long sad time—and now she knew just how bad and sad it was. Was going to be. Unless she was lucky, and she'd never had much luck.

Just the once, she'd been lucky. So lucky. Maybe that was all she had a right to expect, all anybody could expect. For there had been that one golden time. Six whole beautiful happy years, and Mother Ruth, and Sharon, and Danny. She'd had three loves and six years of joy, and that was all, and probably more than a lot of people ever had.

Before, it had been a dark tunnel, stretching away back as far as she could remember, and afterward she'd gotten into the tunnel again, only it seemed so much darker because then she'd been out in the sunlight.

Away back, where any memory at all began, different faces, different voices, a jumble of change. About the farthest, first memory was a woman's sharp voice, "Well, your own mother didn't want you, went away and left you, and now I know why—bad girl! Naughty!" More different faces, different places, and then somehow, an unspecified time later, she was aware that she was owned by something called Social Services, which was a variety of people seen at intervals, who sent her here and there at unscheduled times. To what they called foster homes.

She stayed some places a little while, other places longer. At most places there were other kids from Social Services. She never could remember all the names of the people, in which order they came, how long she stayed, except the places she'd stayed longest.

She stayed with Mrs. Gorman quite a long time, and that was confusing and sometimes uncomfortable, but sometimes fun. Mrs. Gorman was big and fat and red-faced, and she really liked the kids —there were five besides Eileen, all owned by Social Services—but she had an awful temper. One minute she was hugging; the next, spanking. And everybody had to remind her about the first Tuesday of the month, when the inspector always came. She would be in an awful state, panting and grumbling around, "More trouble than it's worth, not that I'd know where to make that much at anything else, a measly hundred for each of you, and Lordy, Lord, that lady finds the beds not made and dirty dishes—and mercy, that bathroom floor never did get done—" Everybody had to help, but sometimes the inspector was mad and said things, and finally she got so mad one day about the kitchen sink that she took them all away from Mrs. Gorman, back to Juvenile Hall, where intervals passed now and then.

The only other place she'd stayed very long was with the Gordons, and that was just the opposite of Mrs. Gorman. There were three other girls owned by Social Services there, Alice and Terry and Sara. You weren't allowed to talk much, or go into the living room, and you had to do all the work in the house, dishes and floors and cleaning the toilet. Then something had happened, Eileen hadn't understood it then, but later on she knew, of course—Mr. Gordon doing *that* to Alice, and the inspector coming with a policeman. And Juvenile Hall again, for quite a while.

A lot of the foster homes didn't want what were called older children, she learned. She never understood why, because the older ones at least didn't make messes or need so much looking after as the little ones. But one thing you couldn't help doing was growing. At that point, she was just thinking that sometime she'd get to be eighteen and wouldn't belong to Social Services any more, and she could go anywhere she wanted and get a job and a room all to herself where she could be alone.

And all that time, every now and then, she had the Dream. At first it was just terror; and then she had come to realize that it was a kind of preview, of something ahead, waiting.

But when she was thirteen, the wonderful lucky thing happened. It had to be the most tremendous luck anyone had ever had, because how many girls were there owned by Social Services, who might have been picked instead? But it was Eileen who went to Mrs. Kruger. To Mother Ruth.

Mother Ruth had two daughters of her own, but they were married and lived a long way off, Colorado and Utah, and she said she was lonesome for a child in the house again. She was kind and jokey and comfortable, she talked a blue streak, while Daddy Kruger just sat and smoked and nodded at her. She taught Eileen all sorts of things she'd never known about—everything she knew now about housework and table manners and proper grammar, and how to behave every way, but Mother Ruth never scolded, teaching, just said, "No wonder you didn't know, child, but now you do, so don't forget it." And because she was the best person in the world, Eileen wanted to be just like her, and she didn't forget. Not anything.

Mother Ruth took her to church for the first time in her life. She could remember now, with new cynicism, what a tremendous reassurance it had been to be told that there was an all-powerful God watching out for her, and His perfect son the Lord Jesus, always ready to answer prayers and keep her from all harm—if she was good. She'd been a fervent believer then, even though Mother Ruth joked about it a little—just a little. "You know, I was raised Methodist myself, and goodness knows they're strict enough, or were then. These Word of God folk, that's Mr. Kruger's church so I've gone to it, but I think sometimes they take themselves a bit too serious, so to speak."

But so much else—so much, the one clear time, she always thought of it, the one happy time. There was Sharon. She'd never had a best friend before. Sharon, wanting Eileen for best friend, all through junior and senior high school. Eileen had gone to so many different schools, it was a wonder she'd learned anything, but she'd always loved to read, and she got good grades mostly, except in math. And that was where Danny came in. Sharon's big brother, but he was nice, he used to help them with their math homework because he was a genius at it, he was going to be an engineer.

And Miss Kingsley, the art teacher—somehow, in all the jumble of the confused years, that had always been Eileen's one solace, drawing things. Whenever she had paper and pencil. Miss Kingsley, keeping her after class, saying, "You show real talent, Eileen. Have you ever thought of going in for commercial art? If you had professional teaching—" Mother Ruth, everybody, admiring her drawings, saying how clever, how pretty.

But it was over in such a little while—six long, beautiful years, eternity while it lasted, so short, looked back on. Dating Danny, while Sharon was dating Dave Long. The Redferns didn't go to the Word of God church, they were Congregationalists, but pretty strict too, and neither she nor Sharon was allowed to date until they were sixteen. Eileen had never dated anybody except Danny, and from the first they both knew it was serious, nobody else would ever be right for either of them. They got engaged when Eileen was eighteen and Danny was twenty, and Mother Ruth said they were awfully young but they couldn't be married for a long while and it was a good family, Danny a nice boy.

He gave her a ring the night she and Sharon graduated from high school. It was just a little ring, a little chip of a diamond in the thin gold band, because Danny only had a part-time job at the college bookstore, but she loved it. It was her very best thing.

They were engaged for six months, and by then Social Services didn't own her any more, Mother Ruth wasn't getting the hundred dollars every month, but it didn't matter, because they belonged to each other then, she had a real family. Danny was in second year in college, and Eileen had a job at Woolworths downtown. When Danny got his degree, they'd be married.

Sharon wasn't engaged to Dave, just going steady. She was going to business school, typing and shorthand. That was the very last of the good golden time, with all of love and beautiful life to look forward to, to last forever. Happy ever after.

And then the doctor said Mother Ruth had to have an operation. There was a tumor. It was on a Tuesday she had the operation, all in a hurry, and they'd had a double date set up for that night. Danny had said he'd pick her up at seven-thirty, but she and Daddy Kruger had to go to the hospital. They'd seen Mother Ruth that afternoon, drowsy and trying to joke at them— "Think they got me tied down here, I'll fool 'em—be home in no time—" And so she'd said to Danny, pick her up at eight-thirty. And so she hadn't been with them in Danny's old car when the other car, speeding out of control, ran into them and both cars caught fire and all of them died.

When they'd been dying—too quick, in the roaring flames—the doctor had been telling Daddy Kruger how Mother Ruth was dying. Cancer, he said. All through her. Maybe six months. In God's hands.

And for the first time, in numb despair, Eileen had thought, God's hands? They said a just God—but that kind of God wouldn't, couldn't do things like this.

She had liked the Redferns—they were kind, happy people. Kind to her, Sharon's friend, Danny's girl. She had thought maybe she could talk to Mrs. Redfern about the awful black despair. But at the funeral—ashes, the minister said, and dust, but how could a person like Danny, a person like Sharon, be suddenly nothing?—happy, laughing people, thinking seriously about things, planning—If God had anything to do with it, she didn't understand Him, or want to love Him. There was only Daddy Kruger with her at the funeral. And afterward, she went up to the Redferns', and Mrs. Redfern said to her in a loud, hard voice, "I don't want to *look* at you! You're still alive!"

So Eileen had had nothing.

Once, oh, once she had been lucky. And now all over again, three and a half years later, she was wishing achingly, sickly, that she had died with Danny and Sharon. She should have been with them. All this misery saved—

Such terrible trouble. Eileen knew now how terrible. Just what the Dream had meant.

Because she had remembered—suddenly and awfully, while the policewoman was talking to her, she had remembered what had happened. Up to where there had been a kind of explosion in her mind—

Wesley didn't understand, you could think he ought to, but that was just futile. Didn't understand how it had been taking care of the old woman. Twenty-four hours a day. Eileen, I want you. Go to the bathroom again. Eileen, I want you. My hymns on the phonograph. Eileen, I want you. Read to me, dear, the book's so heavy. Eileen—

Those awful, awful records of hymns. The hyms she'd once sung joyously, believing. (This morning in church—everybody so horrified, but she couldn't help—) But the choir on the records so mournful, slow, dragging the music out dully.

Eileen, I want you. The book of long, dull sermons, revered and reread because they were written by her father, the Reverend William Penthurst.

Eileen, I want you.

She had seen it all as if it were projected on a screen.

Those *damned* curtains. She hated sewing, she'd never been any good at it, but the bedroom curtains were in shreds. No money, never any money, the old woman never offered any of hers— Cafe rods, she'd just have to measure and put in a hem, and the material had been on sale at Kress's—that was the first time she'd been out of the house in months, Miss Meecham came to stay with the old woman.

She had been settled down—the old woman. Nobody had stayed after church. Wesley was worried about the trouble in the church— if the deacons were annoyed—and some trouble about the job, too. He hadn't wanted any lunch, she'd fixed the old woman's and thought she was settled down, over a book. Start on the curtains. She had just measured carefully, forty-five inches allowing for the hem, and started to cut, when the high, fretful voice rose. "Eileen, I want you!"

And there had been an explosion in her mind, all she could think. *No! Too much! Enough!* She saw herself standing rigid there with the scissors in her hand, and then the screen went blank dark.

But she knew. She knew what must have happened.

She didn't know what time it was when the police went away. She'd been sitting on the church steps, and it was very cold; she was shaking with the cold. She got up slowly and walked back to the house. Wesley was standing on the porch. She said, "We haven't had anything to eat."

"I don't want anything," he said.

She looked at him and thought impersonally, probably he had loved her, in a way. His mother. Maybe the way I loved Mother Ruth, it doesn't seem likely, but he could have.

"Eileen?" he said. "I don't understand—why you left her alone. You never left her."

There wasn't any answer. But quite suddenly, unexpected revelation hit her. She could sleep—sleep all night long! Nobody to wake her three, four, five times a night—Eileen, I want you—she could sleep just as long as she wanted tonight—

CHAPTER 3

Neither of them heard the alarm on Monday morning, and Varallo was late at the office; it was twenty to nine when he got there. Delia was just sliding a triple carbon form out of her typewriter. "Initial report on Endicott," she said succinctly. A very efficient girl at the paperwork, Delia.

"We had another heist last night," Jeff Forbes informed him. "Pharmacy on Central. The clerk's coming in to look at some mug shots."

"Happy day," said Varallo. "We'll need a formal statement from Endicott on finding the body, identification, and so on."

"I called him," said Delia. "He's coming in. I had to tell him where the police station is. I suppose we ought to hear something from the lab on it today."

"No bets."

O'Connor came in, looking distraught. His tie was already under one ear, his shirt rumpled. "I swear to God," he said, "I don't know how people live through it, if they're all like this. A time bomb, 2 A.M. I got a little sleep before, but it's enough to drive a man nuts, for God's sake. Katy says he sleeps like a log most of the day."

"You'll live through it," said Varallo.

O'Connor flung himself down at his desk and gave him a glance of burning resentment. "I don't understand how you deserve it— another one that doesn't keep you awake all night. Goddamn it, there's nothing fair about it." He ran a distracted hand through his curly black hair. Varallo laughed, and Delia smothered a giggle. "Sure, sure, it's so goddamned funny! I'm supposed to be a brain-worker, for God's sake, and I'm so short on sleep I couldn't add two figures together! I swear I'll move out and live at the YMCA until he learns to sleep at night. And the damn dog sounding off as soon as he does—Oh go on, laugh!" He lit a cigarette moodily. His eyes were all bloodshot.

The desk buzzed Varallo, and he picked up the phone. "Yes, Al?"

"Hardware store on Glendale says they've just taken a phony twenty. I'd have shunted them to the Secret Service, but the lieutenant's been on that too, I know, and I thought—"

"Yes indeedy, I'll pass it on. Address?" Varallo passed it on to O'Connor, who swore and picked up his phone.

"None of our damned business, except that this ring seems to be based here." In the past couple of months a respectable sum in the phony twenty-dollar bills had showed up, all at retail stores within the city, never in the same place. "Bunch of idiots," said O'Connor. "I'm damned if I know why they go to the bother. The money the government prints is damned near as phony, pretty paper, and not worth much more. Get me the Hollywood Secret Service office, Al. And nobody, but nobody who took any of it can give us any kind of description at all, but sorting out—Mr. Downs, please—sorting out what they do give us, it's several somebodies, which of course figures —Downs? O'Connor. You've got another funny bill. Just reported. I'll give you the address, you can go waste some more time—"

Katz came in looking preoccupied, sat down at his desk, and said "Good afternoon" to Varallo.

"We missed the alarm."

"There was a pretty moon," said Katz. "I am having a very funny idea about these vandalisms."

"It looked like the same one? That is funny," said Delia.

"It did indeed. Another one," Katz nodded to Varallo's raised brows. "Reported an hour ago. I've just been looking, and it's a carbon copy. Has anybody got an almanac?"

The vandalisms had been getting reported since August—a specialized type of vandalism. Nobody had thought much about the first one—vandalism of all sorts was all too common; but when the second and third and fourth ones came along, they'd taken more interest, done a little work on it. This one would make it a dozen or so, ears damaged, left in unlocked private garages overnight. "An almanac," said Varallo. "You think we should look for X in the stars?"

There wasn't any other way to look: no prints, no physical evidence at the scenes besides the obvious damage.

"Just maybe," said Katz seriously. His thin, dark face wore a sober expression. He got out a cigarette and his notebook. "I've been having a look back over it. Things always coming along, half a dozen things to work at once, all of us doubling in brass, who remembers actual dates? But it just came to me, looking at this one—William Lamprey, Spencer Street, a practically new Dodge, windshield and headlights smashed—that it's been pretty regular, and I looked up the dates. And it's very funny, but it averages out exactly—one every fourteen–fifteen days."

"You don't say," said Varallo. "That is funny, Joe. I only went out on a couple, but it's the same joker, all right."

"Yep. And you know something else?" said Katz. "I think when we look at an almanac it's going to tell us all those dates coincide with the moon."

"The moon!" said O'Connor.

"New moon and full moon. It does set some people off," said Katz. "Ask anybody ever worked at a mental asylum. There was a full moon last night."

"I'll be damned," said Varallo. "That is a thing. But it doesn't give us any handle."

Delia was looking interested. "I heard the chief of detectives say that once. That it isn't just a superstition."

"It's an interesting idea," said O'Connor, "but it doesn't tell you anywhere to go."

Sergeant Duff phoned from the desk to say that the pharmacy clerk was on the way up, and somebody named Endicott. Forbes got up to meet the clerk and take him to look at pictures down in Records. As he went out, Wesley Endicott came in uncertainly. Varallo introduced him to O'Connor and Katz, settled him in the chair beside his desk. Delia had already typed out a brief formal statement from Varallo's notes, and Varallo asked him to read it, take his time, sign it if it was correct.

"Oh yes. Yes, certainly." Endicott was wearing the same rather shabby navy suit, white shirt, and navy bow tie he'd had on last night. He took the pen Varallo offered. Endicott looked white and tired. "I called Mr. Guiterman—explained why I couldn't be at work. Though actually it's only convention—nothing I can do. He was annoyed, that is, he said he was sorry, but— I missed work on Saturday too, I wasn't feeling at all well. I hope those motorcyclists didn't show up again today, they've been coming around a good many Mondays, and they just terrify Barney—he's an elderly man, of course, Mr. Guiterman just calls him in when I can't be there—well, they terrify me, and it's very dangerous." He adjusted his glasses, read over the statement, and signed it. "Have you—have you found out anything?"

"It's early, Mr. Endicott. We don't know yet what the lab may have picked up. I'd better explain to you, the coroner's office will notify you when the body can be released, so you can make arrangements."

"The funeral," said Endicott. "I ought to—I don't think I could—" He looked suddenly ghastly.

"Tell me, has there been any disturbance in the general neighborhood there lately, any trouble—prowlers?"

Endicott shook his head. "No. Trouble—oh my God, yes, *trouble*. And I'm afraid it's going to mean—it just brought everything to a head—of course, Mother didn't *mean*, she didn't *realize*—but everyone, nearly everyone so angry at her and most of them at me, and if the board of deacons—I don't know *what* might come of it, because they haven't been pleased with me, with what I've done here—But I'm sorry, you won't be interested in that—"

"Well, I think maybe we are," said Varallo, regarding him alertly. "Who was angry at your mother? Why?"

"The congregation." Endicott stammered slightly on the word. "Of course, I expect it was my fault, though she—I don't know what else I could have done, I always try to do the right thing, and then it turns out—"

"Just what happened?" Varallo offered him a cigarette, and wasn't surprised when Endicott said he didn't smoke.

"It put me in a difficult position. The way our church operates, we believe in very simple rituals, on the lines of the early Christian gatherings, no complex organization—each pastor is quite on his own, we don't have deacons or elders, just the board of deacons at church headquarters in Sacramento— I explained that we're a small sect. It was all—left up to me, no one to advise or—or back me up—it hasn't been easy. I didn't realize it would be— They were all so used to the old pastor, he'd had this church for years, and people don't like change. And we're supposed to bring new converts in, build up the church, and I haven't been able somehow—and then when Mrs. Lacey did bring that woman in, unfortunately I offended her, and several people said—"

"Which of them were angry at your mother and why?" asked Varallo patiently.

Endicott had a nervous Adam's apple that bobbed up and down. "I daresay it was my fault. I said we're supposed to bring new people in, try to win souls. I'm afraid I've offended some people—but you have to try, if you profess any devotion to God—but some people— Well, you know there are a lot of people who park regularly at that lot, people from the stores and offices all around there, that come in every day. And all the other people who come to park. I always keep a supply of tracts to hand out, and some people got annoyed and complained to the stores that have validated parking there, and they told Mr. Guiterman. He said—but of course you have to expect to sacrifice for the cause. This wasn't anything to do with that, it was Mr. McClintock—he has the shoe-shine stand in front of the barbershop on Broadway. He parks in the lot every day, and I'd talked to him several times. He's just lost his wife, and of course it's part of my duty as a pastor to, er, offer consolation. I invited him to the church, I invited him several times, and then he came. He came," said Endicott, and drew a long breath. "It was a week ago yesterday. It was a dreadful scene—dreadful. I never imagined—"

"What happened?" asked Delia, as if she really wanted to know.

He turned to her, blinking. "I was pleased he'd come, at first. But after—after the service, when I came down to, er, greet people and so on, Mother—I should have known how she'd feel, I just didn't think ahead—she just spoke up to him right there, in front of everybody, and said he didn't belong there, we'd never had any—oh dear, she said 'niggers'—in the church and didn't want any, and—and so on," said Endicott wretchedly. "I was embarrassed, she shouldn't have—but that was the way she would do it, of course, right out like that; I'm afraid she wasn't always tactful—"

That was the understatement of the week, thought Varallo, exchanging a glance with Delia. "And then what happened? What did McClintock do?"

"Oh it wasn't him," said Endicott. Suddenly he shut his eyes, and his small mouth screwed up in distaste. "He just left. It was the rest of them. Most people had heard her, and there was a terrible scene —I never would have imagined—people supposed to be Christians— most of them thought she'd done something terrible, so rude, but some of them—Mrs. Clifford and the Meechams and some others— agreed with her, they were all actually shouting at each other, right in church, it was disrespectful, and I couldn't get them to listen to me at all. And Mr. Haskell said the board of deacons ought to hear about it—and all this past week it's been one thing after another, all of them coming at me for a—an official statement over it—it's all been so awkward— And our only Sunday school teacher resigning; of course, there's only the one class, four children. People calling, coming to the house—not all of them realized I hold another job— Eileen said, coming to see me and getting Mother upset again—just making her more stubborn about it."

"I can see that," said Varallo. "Now I'd like to ask you about something else, Mr. Endicott. That check of your mother's. She had a good bit of money invested in mutual funds?"

Endicott nodded. "I think it's more than a hundred thousand dollars. My father left it to her, he'd inherited it." He didn't question their right to ask him anything; his mind seemed to be off somewhere else, and he answered automatically. "I don't remember him, he died when I was two—he was a lot older than Mother, and she was nearly forty when I was born. He had tuberculosis, they were always afraid I'd have it too, I was ill a good deal when I was younger."

"Are there any other relatives? You'll be her heir?"

"Oh no, there isn't any family left. Yes, I think she made a will," said Endicott vaguely. He stood up, hovered there looking miserable. "I—it all just made me realize I've been a failure—a failure as a pastor. I thought I had a call—I tried—but they haven't accepted me—

and no new members in three years, and the board of deacons— But I'm sorry, of course that can't have anything to do with—with what happened. I just hope you can find out—but of course as a Christian one mustn't want any revenge—" He was unsure how to get himself away; finally he went out, and they heard him stumble on the stairs.

"Well, that is a piece of limp string," said O'Connor. "And could that have anything to do with what happened to Mother? Self-righteous old bitch she must've been. These good Christians. If you ask me, this McClintock might have taken it into his head to biff her one."

"A week later?" said Varallo. "Oh I want to talk to him all right."

Delia sat back in her chair and lit a cigarette. "That," she said in her deep voice, "is just what he looks like—a piece of damp, chewed string. How in the world that girl ever got involved with him—quite a pretty girl, though there's something a little funny about her too. Maybe just shock. Maybe not. But I'm wondering if that isn't just the effect the innocent young pastor means to make. Whether he— or both of them—hadn't gotten tired of tactless Mother, too tight even to buy a pair of new curtains, and making trouble in the congregation."

Varallo shook his head at her. "Scissors," he said. "Nobody planned it."

"There is that. But it still could be. One or the other of them," said O'Connor.

As if on cue, Burt came in and put a plastic evidence bag on Varallo's desk. The scissors were in it. "Goulding sent them over first thing. Just like I said, nothing but smudges. Just ordinary scissors, a couple of bucks at any dime store. I suppose somebody can say if they came from the house."

"Anything else?"

"Give us time," said Burt. "We're still sorting out prints." He went out.

"Well, at least this gives us some places to look and people to see," said Varallo. "Trouble in the congregation."

"But that's no sort of motive," said Delia. "I can't see—"

O'Connor and Varallo both laughed a little grimly. "When you've seen as many homicides as the rest of us, you'll know better," said

O'Connor. "Reason the D.A. doesn't have to show motive legally. There's no such thing as a good motive for homicide—what is a motive depends on who has it. And just the little I've heard about this, and considering the weapon—as Vic just pointed out—nobody planned to kill her. Sounds to me as if somebody just lost his temper, grabbed up the handiest tool, and let fly."

"Yes," said Varallo, "and was just lucky there wasn't any witness, that she didn't make any noise. But there could have been noise, at that. The church in front—and Central's a busy street even on Sunday—and all the windows closed in that apartment." He ran an absent hand through his crest of tawny gold hair. "People coming," he said thoughtfully. "To see Endicott, and staying to tell her how they felt. And righteous Christian principles have, you could say, caused a lot of homicides in the past."

O'Connor grinned his sharklike grin. "Haven't they just. Tactless Mother. I can see one of those parishioners, all shocked at Mother's lack of brotherly love, turning up there and getting into an argument with her and just seeing red for one second."

"We'd better have a look at them anyway," agreed Varallo. "I suppose there'll be a list of church members somewhere."

Katz had disappeared sometime ago, and now came back with a thick book in his hand. "Found one at that paperback store up on Brand. I was right. On the button, every one of these vandalisms was on a night of new moon or full moon."

"Interesting but useless," said O'Connor through a yawn.

———◄◆►———

As Varallo and Delia came downstairs into the lobby, Sergeant Alfred Duff was just unplugging a wire in the switchboard. "These damn young punks," he said. "I hope Traffic catches up and throws the book at them. This motorcycle gang again."

"Motorcycles?" said Varallo.

"Oh not Hell's Angels. Just a bunch of young punks. We've had forty, fifty complaints just the past month. Half a dozen kids on the souped-up bikes, making a speedway out of lower Maryland and Broadway, and skidding all around the parking lots down there. They nearly killed one woman in that alley between Wilson and

Broadway. They're out again—it's usually in the mornings—the attendant at the bank lot just called, and I chased Judovic and Stein over."

"Look," said Varallo to Delia, "I'll see if I can locate McClintock. Save time, suppose you see if you can get a list of the parishioners, and maybe an ident on the scissors." Conceivably, Burt could find a print that matched up with a known violent daylight burglar in Records, though it wasn't very likely; he still thought this one was going to end up in Pending; but while they had any lead, however faint, it had to be followed up. Delia agreed amiably, and drove off in the old Mercedes. Varallo headed down to Broadway and turned right up to Maryland.

As he waited for the light at the corner, to make a left for that parking lot, he heard the motorcycles in the distance, roaring away. In the parking lot itself, which backed up to the row of stores and offices on Broadway, two black-and-whites faced each other at sharp angles; Judovic and Stein were wrestling with a big lout of a kid, just hauling him up to his feet, slapping on the cuffs. There was a parallel parking slot at the curb, and Varallo slid the Gremlin into it. Apparently one of the punks had offered resistance, and would be due for more than a moving violation ticket. As he walked back toward Broadway, both cars were pulling out of the lot, leaving the lot attendant—Barney?—contemplating a motorcycle lying in the middle of a parking space.

The barber shop was open. Outside its narrow entrance was a single shoe-shine chair. There was a solid-looking elderly black man sitting in it, reading a newspaper. He looked about sixty; he had a round bald head and beefy shoulders. "Mr. McClintock?" said Varallo.

The paper came down. "That's me. What can I do for you?"

————————◆————————

Delia waited a long time on the tiny wooden porch, wondering if anyone was here; Endicott might still be waiting for a bus. When the door finally opened, Eileen faced her sleepily. She had a blue corduroy robe on, and old black house slippers.

"I'm sorry to disturb you," said Delia.

"It was time I got up." Eileen was a little flushed with sleep like a child, and, Delia thought, really quite a pretty girl. "Do you want to come in?" Eileen stepped back.

The wheelchair was still there, pushed in front of the couch. Delia sat down in the green chair, opened her bag, and took out the scissors. "Can you tell me if these are yours? Belong to the house, that is?"

Eileen looked at them steadily. "They're the ones— Yes, I think so. Just like the ones here, anyway."

"I think," said Delia, "you were using a pair of scissors—these or another pair—just before you went out yesterday, weren't you? Cutting some material in your bedroom."

"Oh yes. I was."

"With these scissors?"

"They're just like the ones I was using. The only scissors in the house, I think."

"What did you do with them when you left?"

The girl was much calmer, steadier today. Her eyes met Delia's openly. "Why, I left them there. I hadn't finished cutting out the curtains for the bedroom. I left them on the bed, I guess. On the material."

"You must have left in rather a hurry. Right in the middle of cutting it."

Eileen was silent and then said, "Why yes. It was so hot. Mrs. Endicott was settled down with her book—I wanted some fresh air."

"We've been hearing from your husband about what happened at the church last week."

"Oh yes."

"How did you feel about it?"

"Me?" said Eileen, a little surprised. "Well, Wesley ought to have known better, but of course it's the sort of thing he would do. Mrs. Endicott had a lot of prejudices. She didn't like black people, or Italians, or Jews, or people who drink and smoke. Or cats," she added suddenly. "And of course she would say all that in front of everybody. She didn't mind being rude to people, she called it being forthright and not shilly-shallying. I was so sorry for the poor man—

but he was the only one who, well, kept any dignity. He just walked out, and then everybody started to shout and argue."

"Did you take any part in it?"

"Oh it wouldn't have been any use my saying anything, I don't think most of them like me very well either." She laughed, and sobered. "After I got to laughing that first time— I couldn't help it, it just suddenly struck me so funny, you know, all of them—*soldiers of the Cross*—old Mr. Haskell with his fat stomach and Mrs. Meecham with her cane and Mrs. Lane with her wig—and every time Wesley called for it again I'd get to laughing—"

After a moment Delia asked her for a list of church members. "Oh yes, Wesley keeps one—it'll be with the church papers in the vestry." Eileen got up, took a key from a box on an end table, and led Delia over to the church. Involuntarily, in the chill air of the ugly little building, Delia shivered, eyeing the grim text. There didn't seem to be many church papers, in a small square chest in a sort of alcove inside the double front doors. Eileen found the list and gave it to her, three typewriter-size sheets. Eileen didn't show any curiosity as to why they wanted it, ask any questions. She let Delia out the front door; when Delia glanced back, walking around to the driver's door of the car at the curb, Eileen was still standing there at the top of the steps, looking down at the key in her hand.

Eileen locked the church and crossed the little space of brown grass to the house. She was feeling now as if she was a little way off from everything, and at the same time seeing everything in clearer perspective than ever before, able to look at everything with utter calm.

She wondered where Wesley was. She didn't much care. Anybody might have thought, knowing all about it, that she would blame Wesley for everything—it would have been easy to do—the way he had tricked her, the things they had both done, he and the old woman. But she never had blamed him, because of course it had been her own fault in the beginning.

Suddenly, standing on the porch, she smiled. The cat had come again: the plump gray cat that had belonged to the old minister who died. Mrs. Eddy across the street had taken the cat: his name was Smokey. Eileen sat down on the porch and called softly, and the cat came to her and rubbed against her knee. It was very queer to think that long, long before the cat had been born, he'd been in her Dream, again and again.

That had been another thing Mother Ruth had given her. Animals. Eileen had never touched an animal in her life before she was with Mother. But Mother Ruth always had a cat. Blackie had been old when Eileen came, and he died when she was fourteen, and then they got Boxer, the fat tabby kitten who sat up and boxed at you with big six-toed front feet, and grew into an enormous cat with great yellow eyes. All the rest of her life Eileen would be fascinated by cats, the grace and beauty and independence, and the thrumming purr you could feel all warm through the fur. And the Redferns had had a dog, such a nice dog, a big black-and-white dog named Freckles.

She held the cat, stroking it gently, and she wondered how the cat had gotten in yesterday. He always did try to get into the house, his old home, if he was anywhere around.

She looked at the cat and thought she'd like to try to draw a picture of him. Anything alive was always harder to draw so it looked real— She hadn't tried to draw anything for a long time. Well, she hadn't had time—in a long time—to do anything but housework and taking care of the old woman. But even when she'd just thought about drawing, somehow they'd made an ugly picture in her mind, she didn't want to think about it.

She hadn't really known either of them, of course. Anything about them. That was why it was her fault—she had been so foolish, so stupid. Back then, the old woman still getting around, helping in the house; Eileen could go out sometimes. There was an art store uptown, right at the main corner, Aaron Brothers, where there were hundreds of pictures to look at; she liked to go there. They hadn't been here very long then, that night she'd been trying to copy a sketch she'd seen there; the old woman asked about it, said how nice, dear, seemed interested, so Eileen had brought out all her drawings,

all her best ones she'd kept in a big manila envelope. And there had
been the ones of Sharon—

Sharon, so lovely, slim and white-skinned and graceful as a cat—all
the art books Eileen had gotten out of the library, trying all the
different styles and subjects—Sharon, staying over with Eileen or the
other way around when they did homework together—

The old woman's ugly hands ripping and tearing at the paper.
"Vile—wicked—wouldn't have thought you capable of such a thing!
I thought you were a modest girl—a lady!" And Wesley so shocked,
his little mouth pinched, bundling the paper out to the trash can.
All her drawings of Sharon—Miss Kingsley had said, good line, my
dear, they're really very good— Eileen had been more astonished
than angry then.

They wouldn't even talk about it. "But Wesley, it says in the
Bible that God created man in His own image. If that's so, there
can't be anything sinful about just bodies—"

"You don't understand these things."

Of course, she wasn't surprised about Wesley. Not by then. Oh so
easy to blame him, blame them, for tricking and trapping her—but
she needn't have been. She'd made the choice, being so stupid.

It was very queer, how the reality of the Dream happening at last
had given her a kind of release. Now she knew the Dream would
never come again, because it had happened at last and she knew
what it meant, she felt free and light. She seemed to have emerged
halfway out of the dark tunnel again and could look back with
clearer understanding, how she'd gotten into it at all.

Ministers talked about people falling into error. That was what
had happened to her—she'd fallen into black error, out of the despair and grief after the accident, and Mother Ruth dying, and
Daddy Kruger so old, broken, and helpless.

She should have known there was something queer about it. Not
natural. She hadn't lived through Juvenile Hall and all the foster
homes without learning all the worst cusswords there were and everything there was to know about sex. But all of the real times of her
life—the only important times—had been with Mother Ruth, and
Eileen had believed all the things the minister said, and all the ugly

things she knew had gotten buried deep, not to be thought about. She only knew it would be right and beautiful with Danny, when it came, when they were married.

But after the accident, with Mother Ruth dying faster every day, it was as if any feeling or sense or judgment Eileen had was frozen tight in the ice of despair. Daddy Kruger went to the church a lot. Long habit took Eileen there on Sunday, but it didn't mean anything now. They knew people at church; they knew the Endicotts, Mrs. Endicott a fixture, prominent member, her father one of the founders, and she was supposed to be rich. Young Mr. Endicott, soon to be ordained a pastor. They were known faces, that was all. It surprised Eileen immensely when Wesley asked her to go out with him one Sunday. She wasn't interested, didn't want to go; but Daddy Kruger had overheard, said she ought to. "You're young, girl, I forget how young—you can't look back, got your whole life before you."

It wasn't like a date. He didn't know what to say to her, how to act. He asked her out again, and again. Then, Mother Ruth was back in the hospital. She was dying when Wesley asked Eileen to marry him, and she sat by the bed holding her hand and told her about it. The ice was all around her. All there was room for in her mind was that again she was going to be left, abandoned, to be all alone with nobody who loved her. She had lived all her life with that knowledge, before Mother Ruth, and she was deathly afraid to live that way again.

"So surprised," she said. "He didn't seem—I don't know—" The hand in hers was so thin, so cold.

"It's a good family," said Mother Ruth, sounding surprised too. And when she got enough breath again, "At least you'd be safe, child. Settled. I could—rest easy—about you. Worry about you—you're too thin-skinned." And a long while later, drowsily, "Young—you wouldn't forget Danny—but you'll get past it. A whole life to live."

She had died before the doctor expected her to, very suddenly, the next day—they hadn't been with her, she'd just slipped away.

Now, this time later, looking back and seeing clearly, Eileen thought that very likely Mother Ruth had meant, your whole life to live, don't do anything in a hurry, think about it and be sure. She'd never know.

But Danny was dead, and so nothing mattered, what happened to Eileen didn't matter, except that everybody she loved had gone away and left her and she was alone. Daddy Kruger had always been in the background, vague.

She couldn't cry at the funeral. It was a dressed-up doll in the coffin, not her first love, not Mother Ruth.

Mother Ruth had said, you'd be safe, I could rest easy. So she told Wesley she would marry him. It didn't really matter.

So it had all been her own fault, everything that had happened.

Very soon she found how Wesley had tricked her, and why. And even that had been mostly the old woman's fault. So proud of him, a pastor with his own church—

Pillars of the church, thought Eileen dreamily, stroking the cat, feeling the lovely purr. Hadn't known either of them—just faces in church. When she did, she didn't like either of them. Mrs. Endicott —she'd just been a neat, nicely dressed, polite old lady talking to people after the service, smiling, seeming to be a pleasant old lady. Wesley, nervously correct and polite, what he looked like didn't matter after Danny, but he hadn't started to lose his hair then, and his eyes were young and anxious— Suddenly the cat got up, stretched, and left her. He stalked across the brown grass, paused at the curb, and ran across the street. Cats didn't have any sentimentality. You couldn't constrain them to be loving when they didn't feel like it.

Just as suddenly Eileen thought she'd like to talk to Marcella Moore. She could. She could go anywhere she wanted. It was so long since she'd been free to do that, the very thought made her feel like a balloon, slightly dizzy, floating a little way up. She could do whatever she wanted. She had a couple of dollars in her purse, bus fare. She could—

———◆———

With five years as a policewoman with LAPD—even though she'd been stationed in Hollywood mostly, not the inner city—Delia Riordan had heard and seen nearly everything a cop does see on the job.

It could be that anyone who wanted to be a career cop was simply interested in human nature, in people. At least that was one answer.

"—And I tell you, it was one real row!" Mrs. Stella Clifford was saying with some relish. Mrs. Clifford was short and fat, with gray hair and little dark eyes behind thick glasses. She had sprayed information at Delia rapidly, unasked, in between a spate of avid questions and exclamations— "It don't seem possible, saw her at church just yesterday, just like always, in the midst of life, well, that's so, but to think of a thing like that happening—" She was a widow, her two boys lived with her, Stanley still in school but Dexter had a good job driving a truck, brought in good money. She was away now on eager reminiscences of last week, if that was what Delia wanted to hear.

"I got to say, I was real surprised at some people stood up and said it wasn't right—the Haskells and Lanes and Mrs. Beck, most of 'em —it don't make any difference what anybody says, or the government either about the equal rights and all, what I say is, God made everybody and He musta had some reason make them different, they're one sort and we're another, you can't deny that. And I thought Mrs. Endicott did just right to speak out plain like that, tell that black fellow he didn't no ways belong there with the rest of us, and I stood by her and told 'em all I thought so. She—" Mrs. Clifford broke off abruptly at the sound of a door shutting somewhere out of sight. "Stanley! Where you think you're going? You can't go out till you've read the Bible a whole hour, you know that!"

"I did, Ma." He stood in the doorway of the living room, the expectable teen-ager, unkempt hair, jeans, T-shirt. He had a bad case of acne. "I did, honest. I finished Jeremiah."

"All right. Boys!" said Mrs. Clifford. The back door banged shut. This was a drab middle-class apartment on Palmer Street, conventionally furnished, a little untidy, ordinary. "I don't know what gets into 'em. See, I had the flu a couple weeks ago, the minister came to see me, and he found out Stanley had a real dirty book—he wouldn't say where he got it, the minister gave him a talking, and I set him to read the Bible right through. It's hard, raise children the right way."

"I'm sure it must be," said Delia. "You were telling me about the —mmh—dispute in the church."

"I wouldn't've believed it, the way people talked. Saying she was all wrong, talking about being real Christians—and those snippy little chits of girls talking all righteous about hypocrites—that Annie Lane and Caroline Beck, think they'd know better than to talk back to elders and betters. I don't know what their parents are thinking of — But Mrs. Endicott sure turned the tables on 'em, she spoke up real sharp and, I suppose, she says, you're so afraid of being hypocrites, you wouldn't mind my telling what I heard you two talking about in the rest room—oh, you didn't know I was there, did you?—little liars, she says, covering up for each other, probably up to no good with boys, what I can guess— Well!" said Mrs. Clifford, her little eyes sparkling, "you should've heard the Lanes and the Becks then! And the two girls about ready to faint away! Talk about fireworks!"

Delia could imagine it.

CHAPTER 4

They were sitting there at the office kicking things around, toward the end of the shift. The APB's on the two suspected heist men hadn't paid off yet. The clerk from the pharmacy hadn't picked any mug shot, on the heist last night. Katz had had a look in Records and made up a list of possibles, not that there was much individual MO about the average heist; he and O'Connor had one of those in an interrogation room when Varallo came in, and ten minutes later they came out and shooed him off, a sullen, unshaven fellow who went gladly.

"Up in the air, damn it," said O'Connor, and the chair squeaked as he sat down and swiveled it around. "Could be, couldn't be. No alibi." Too many heist jobs, anonymous, never got cleaned up at all.

Forbes was coughing his heart out and cussing. "Damn it, I shouldn't have come in this soon. Conscientious, that's me. Feel as if I'm coming down with the damn thing all over again."

"Well, it's your day off tomorrow." O'Connor scowled at him. "Shedding germs all over the rest of us."

Delia came in, and Forbes said hoarsely, "I'm past the contagious stage. I'm going home to bed—half a dozen aspirin and a few jiggers of Bourbon ought to do something."

Burt came in and said, "I haven't got much for you on Endicott."

"Did you locate McClintock?" asked Delia.

"Oh yes." Varallo blew smoke at the ceiling and laughed. "At least we know he didn't do it. I like Sam McClintock. He's a sane man in a dizzy world."

The solid, stolid-looking McClintock had listened to Varallo soberly; they had talked there standing in front of the shoe-shine stand, people occasionally passing, a customer entering the barber shop. This part of downtown Glendale wasn't as busy, as crowded as it used to be; Brand Boulevard half a block up actually had empty parking spaces to show. The combination of the fire at Webbs' and the new, immense Galleria shopping mall over on Central had shunted shoppers west.

"Now, that's an awful thing to happen," said McClintock. "I wouldn't wish anybody to die like that. He shook his head. "I suppose you want to talk to me on account of what happened at the church."

"Something like that, Mr. McClintock. When we heard about it, we thought you might have felt, shall we say, a little bit annoyed at Mrs. Endicott." This man hadn't snatched up a pair of scissors in blind rage.

McClintock laughed, but his eyes were a little sad. "I reckon I had reason to be, but there's no profit in it, is there? That little fellow, the attendant in the parking lot behind here, he kept on at me, come to his church. Seems funny to think he's a minister with a church, working at a job like that. Not much of a church—I'd never heard of it before. Oh, he's been at everybody around here regular, and some people didn't like it much. Taking his little gospel tracts into Nick's bar and grill at the corner—" McClintock smiled.

"And offering you—er—consolation."

The smile faded. "That's so. Nella and me were married thirty-five years, and it's a fact, I miss her. We all do. But I know she's all right. Can't say I've ever been a regular churchgoer, she went more than me, but I do believe there's something else after a person dies. Don't have to go to church to know that. I'll tell you, Mr. Varallo, the little fellow just kept on at me so persistent, so earnest and all, I thought I'd go once just to gratify him."

Varallo laughed. "And got an unexpected reaction from the good Christians."

McClintock shrugged. "I guess it was mostly that one old lady. I didn't stay to find out. Sure, I didn't feel good about it—who would? But I'll tell you, Mr. Varallo, people like that can't hurt me none, because they can't change what I am inside, can they?" Suddenly he grinned widely, showing even white teeth against his black skin. "It reminds me of the time— See, I just keep this little stand here, give me somethin' to do, I'm retired really—always earned a decent living at a lot of things, trucking, gardenwork, waiting on table, but our three boys, they're doin' a lot better. Steve, he's got his own TV repair business, and Don's with the phone company. I still got the youngest, Lonnie, at home, he's going to college to be a lawyer, all things. But what I was going to say, it kind of reminded me—this old friend of mine, Benny White, he's got a catering business, and times somebody lets him down he ropes me in to help. I'm a pretty good bartender. And a while back, he got this job, a real big bash at a fancy house in Beverly Hills. I dunno if they was movie people or just society. And there was this one dude, a big fat fellow, kept coming back for vodka gimlets. He sure could hold his liquor, I didn't count how many he had, but he was callin' me every name in the book. You goddamn black bastard, he'd say, you black baboon-face, when'd you get down outta the trees? he'd say—and every time he did, he'd slap a sawbuck in my breast pocket." McClintock chuckled. "I come home and told Nella I don't care what he calls me, for that kind of money. Bad-wording can't hurt nobody."

"Drunks," grinned Varallo. "You're a philosopher."

"I'll tell you who was mad—not at the drunk, the old lady—was Lonnie. He was fighting mad. Wanted to come roaring over here and tell those folk off. I told him, let it lay. No point."

Now, relaying all that, Varallo said, "But I suppose I'd better see Lonnie. In case he was still mad."

"And," said Delia, "there's this I just turned up. These girls."

Varallo listened, didn't think much of it. "Isn't anybody interested in what I've got to say?" asked Burt plaintively. "Not that it's much. Most of the prints there were the Endicotts'—all three of 'em. We only made one set different—three dandy latents in the middle of the kitchen door. They're not in our records, I passed them on to LAPD and the FBI. Maybe they'll be in somebody's files."

"And maybe not," said O'Connor. "That's just another anonymous kill we'll never clean up."

Goulding looked in the door. "You'll have a formal autopsy report tomorrow on your latest corpse, but nothing I can't tell you in five minutes. I doubt if there was any planning or skill involved—just the stab wound, and of course with that broad a weapon, closed pair of scissors, he was bound to do some damage. They nicked the heart and ruptured the right ventricle. She couldn't have lived five minutes."

"Time of death?" asked Varallo.

"Now, that I can't pin down very close. I said that damned heater would confuse things. Between 1 and 2 P.M., all I can say. She'd had soup and some kind of sandwich a short time before, but digestions vary—especially old ones. It could have been an hour, even more."

"The girl says she had lunch about one," said Delia. "Any indication that she tried to defend herself? How helpless was she?"

Dr. Goulding shrugged. "Rheumatoid arthritis, fairly well advanced. She'd have been helpless, all right, way you mean it. I don't think she'd have had time to do anything, in that sense. He had gravity on his side, too, it was a downward blow—naturally, she sitting in a wheelchair—and those scissors, a pretty hefty weapon—they went right in without touching a bone. That's about it."

But Eileen hadn't gone to see Marcella Moore. Marcella Moore was very sharp, and might see and guess things.

She owned the dress shop there on Broadway, and she was one of the regulars in that parking lot. Another one Wesley had pressed the invitations on, come to the church. She had come, once, and not again. She was an interesting looking woman, not young but very smart, with gray-black hair and a long sharp nose and big dark eyes. That was before the old woman was in the wheelchair, and Wesley kept urging Eileen to go and see her, trying to persuade her to come — "Make her understand she's welcome, maybe another woman could reach her better—" Reluctantly, she had gone. She didn't want to urge Wesley's God on anybody.

But Marcella Moore had, surprisingly, given God back to Eileen. Listening to her halting, set little speech, half smiling, she had said, "Well, you see, my dear, I came to see what your husband's church was like, but I'm afraid I can't accept such rigid fundamentalism. I've been a reincarnationist for some time."

"I don't know what that is."

"Well, a good many people believe it's what Jesus Christ was talking about. It's really the only logical answer to explain the justice of God. But I don't want to disturb your own faith—"

"Oh, you couldn't," said Eileen. There wasn't any; not since everybody had died. And customers came in, and she left. Those days, she could still go places, and she had gone to the library often. She asked for books on reincarnation, and the librarian told her where to find some. They were the most interesting books she'd ever read, and she thought about them a lot, especially the one called *Many Mansions*. It explained so much she'd never been able to understand about God. And it was all so logical, so much more logical than the last judgment and heaven and hell. If God had just started things off like that, everybody on his own, and always a chance to do better in some next life, He was a just God. He didn't judge or condemn anybody, He just made the rules. You did the deciding, whether you'd done right or wrong, and anything wrong you had to pay for, that was absolutely fair.

It gave her back that ultimate reassurance, that somewhere she'd catch up to them again—Mother Ruth and Sharon and Danny. Probably they'd all been together before, and would be again. Maybe in some next life, she and Danny would have what they'd missed in this one. Maybe they'd both done something very wrong before, and had had to pay for it this time, and that was why. You just had to wait, and know you'd be together again.

She went back and talked with Marcella; they used to go out to lunch together sometimes. Maybe because she'd never had a friend before Sharon (and Sharon had been enough), she wasn't good at making friends. She'd known other girls at school, but they'd lost touch, the relationship tenuous. Now and then she wrote Daddy Kruger, but he only sent a little note with a Christmas card. There wasn't anybody near her age in the church, the only young people a few teen-agers, the four children in Sunday school. Mrs. Meecham's daughter Harriet played the organ for the services, not very well; she was about thirty, but she seemed as old as her mother. But Eileen felt that Marcella was a friend, really liking her for what she was. Really listening to her, interested in her.

"My dear, you're an intelligent reader," Marcella said once. And another time, "You have a sensitive mind."

Of course, eventually Wesley and the old woman discovered what Eileen was reading, and there was all the talk about heathen creeds and wickedness. Their minds closed down *snap*, and you couldn't talk to them. She was never to speak to that wicked woman again. But they couldn't stop her. She told Marcella about it and Marcella laughed, but she looked worried too.

They were having lunch together at the counter in Kress's, and Marcella put down her sandwich and said, "But it's made trouble for you at home, trouble between you and—" She studied Eileen with queer intentness and then said, "And you're only twenty—so young— but you're not a fool. My dear girl, however did you get mixed up with that silly little man? Oh my goodness, that's terribly rude—forgive me."

But true, thought Eileen. That night, looking at him with seeing eyes for the first time in months, she had noticed impersonally how fast his hair was going, how weak and moist his eyes behind the thick glasses. And not long after that, the old woman got much worse, and was in the wheelchair, and after that there just wasn't time to go anywhere, see anyone, read any books, even to do much thinking. Eileen was tired most of the time, if she had a minute to herself she just sat down thankfully.

She hadn't gone to see Marcella today. She didn't know if Marcella was still there, at the dress shop. It was two years since she'd seen her. She took the bus uptown and looked in some windows, bought a sandwich at Kress's.

When she came back, Wesley was there. "Where have you been?"

"Places," said Eileen. Just for the sixteen hours' solid sleep she felt as if she'd come a little way alive, more than she had been in months. She got out what was left of the hamburger, a can of asparagus, the leftover creamed potatoes. Without a qualm she struck a match to light the burners. All her life she'd been nervous of lighting matches, and the old stove had been the worst thing about the new life here. Just now she didn't even think about it.

He sat across from her and picked at the food. He said, "It seems so strange to have Mother—just not here. So suddenly. Doesn't it seem strange? I'll have to arrange for a funeral. They won't like it if I'm off work all day tomorrow too, but I'll have to— There's money to think about. I can't touch any of Mother's—the man at the bank said—I don't know how we'll manage."

There was rice pudding; the old woman always had to have rice pudding. He said he didn't want any. "Everything—all of a sudden," he said. "Mother—and people leaving the church, there wasn't half the usual congregation there. All that bitterness. They've never accepted me—never liked me—that just made me realize it."

Seeing clearly, Eileen thought, and realize something else too, whether he admitted it or not. He had always deferred to the old woman, done what she told him, and for the first time—over that silly little thing—he had been at odds with her, and afraid to let her see it, and it had made him look like a fool to everybody. Which the old woman wouldn't have seen at all—wouldn't have seen, hadn't seen, what she'd done. So proud of my son the minister, his own church.

"Eileen," he said, "Eileen—I still don't understand why you left her alone. Where did you go?"

"Out," said Eileen. "It was the first time I'd been out of the house, except to the church, in nearly six months. Oh, some of the women used to offer to come and sit with her, Mrs. Meecham, Mrs. Haskell, but she didn't like that. I might have had time to do some more wicked drawings, or read wicked books." He stared at her. "You just never thought, did you, how much there was to do. How it was for me here. All the care of her. The house. The washing. There's something wrong with the wringer on the washing machine, it doesn't get all the water out, and the sheets are so heavy." She didn't say it with anger or resentment, just as a fact of life.

"I know it hasn't been easy. So little money—"

"You were just sitting at that lot all day. Taking parking tickets. Or shut up in the bedroom writing sermons." Such dull, disorganized sermons.

"I don't know why it takes me so long to compose a sermon," he said dully. "I worked so hard at divinity school, it was harder for me than most of them, I don't know why. I thought I had a calling, but I realize—just now—it was all Mother's—drive. Insistence. I've been a failure here. I was so proud when the board gave me my own church—that isn't usual when you've just been ordained. I think—I think maybe she gave the board some money, and that was why—"

"And she didn't really want you to get married, but it was more important that you have the church."

"I've never heard you talk like this," he said with a gasp. "Why did you leave her?"

"Because I'd had too much," said Eileen tranquilly. "All of a sudden, it was too much. I suppose we'd both gotten into habits. Calling me to hand her something she could reach. Calling me every ten minutes. And it was easier to come, and do it, than have an argument. And of course she never thought about me. I was just there. Never thought, was I in the middle of doing the dishes or washing my hair. Just a pair of hands to wait on her. And I had had enough." Her voice was remote, cool. She hadn't talked this much to him in months. Ever.

"Eileen!" he said. "You—you sound—as if you hated her. You couldn't—you didn't—*you couldn't have*—"

She glanced at him briefly, getting up, starting to pick up the dishes. There was terrible dread in his pale eyes, and shrinking suspicion. He opened his mouth and then shut it again tightly. He wouldn't ask, he wouldn't voice it, he was afraid, but he was much more afraid to know for certain.

———◆———

At ten-forty the night watch got a call to a homicide. They had just gotten back from another heist job, and the report wasn't typed; they swore resignedly and went out again.

It was one of the jerry-built newish apartments on Pacific Avenue, an upper front, and a sexy-looking young brunette was sobbing all over Patrolmen Gordon and Stoner.

"It's her mother," said Stoner. "She just got home and found her."

Rhys and Hunter looked at the corpse, which was that of a still good-looking middle-aged woman with dark hair and a good figure. She was lying in the middle of the front bedroom floor, and she hadn't a stitch on; it looked as if she'd taken a beating.

"You know, we're damn shorthanded, with business up like this," said Rhys. "Burt and Thomsen were out overtime last night too." But it couldn't be helped. What they got out of the girl, she and her father lived here too—she didn't know where he was, but he'd be coming home—and you couldn't shut people out of their homes. She said her name was Brenda Leeds; the mother was Wilma Leeds, and her father was Dudley.

He hadn't showed up when Rhys and Hunter went back to the office to get out an initial report, leaving Burt and Thomsen, annoyed at being called out, still poking around.

The heist job sounded like another one that had gone down last week, at a liquor store. The owner had made a positive ident on a mug shot, and there was an APB out on that one now: Daniel Ricketts, Caucasian, 24, 6 feet, 160, brown and blue, a package of various felonies and three other heists. The clerk at the dairy store held up at eight-thirty had given them a pretty good description, which sounded as if it could be Ricketts. The day men would be getting him to look at pictures.

At least they didn't get another call until the end of the shift.

———◆———

On Tuesday morning, lacking Forbes, they got John Poor back. Delia wanted to chase up those girls the Clifford woman had mentioned; Varallo said it sounded like a tempest in a teapot. "Though I grant you, on a random one like this, no telling what might have sparked it off. I want to talk to Lonnie." The kickback from the FBI, on that set of prints, hadn't come in yet; they ought to hear from LAPD today.

O'Connor slapped Rhys's report down on Varallo's desk. "And another possibly random one, damn it, which we've got to do some work on. And clean up this latest heist if we can—Hunter says it could have been this Ricketts again. John, you'd better go get that clerk in, see if he can make the mug shot. Why the hell that APB hasn't turned him up—every cop in the county's got his plate number— And I want you," he said to Delia, "to talk to this Leeds girl. She was all to pieces last night, Bob couldn't get anything out of her."

Just then a new call came in, a burglary reported at an address in Whiting Woods, so Poor and Katz went out on that instead.

Varallo escaped before anything else turned up and drove over to Hollywood, to the LACC campus. It had turned colder today, and the forecast said freezing tonight. It would, his day off not until tomorrow. He thought, just hope the roses would all come through the night safe, and tomorrow he'd get them all covered with burlap. The climbing ones would just have to take their chances.

At the registrar's office, he asked for Lonnie McClintock, was directed to a classroom in another wing, and presently faced Lonnie there in the bare corridor. Lonnie was a tall, thin black with inquisitive eyes and a sharp little mustache; he looked at the badge, heard Varallo's name, and nodded.

"Dad was telling me about it last night. About that old bitch getting herself killed. Funny. You don't think we had anything to do with it, do you?"

"I don't think your father did. Did you?" asked Varallo mildly.

"Well, for God's sake," said Lonnie. "For God's sake. I was good and damn mad about it—madder than Dad was, but he's too easygoing for his own good sometimes. It was the damn arrogance got me —the nerve! That—that minister practically dragging him into that damn church, and then that old bitch— How do they figure it, anyway? That's what I'd like to know."

"Figure what?"

"How come they didn't happen to get born a different color? Doesn't seem to be any choice about it. They figure they were just lucky, or what?"

Varallo laughed. "I don't think they do any thinking about it at all. Well, were you mad enough to do anything about it?"

"I tell you, I was all set to go over there and tell that damn minister and the old bitch just what I thought of them, but Dad argued me out of it. He said, what's the point, and of course there wasn't any. You don't change people like that by talk."

"Unfortunately. Where were you Sunday afternoon, say noon to two o'clock?"

"Alibi," said Lonnie. "Sure. You can stop wasting your time. I was at home boning for a Latin exam." Home was a single house in the Atwater district between Hollywood and Glendale.

"Alone?"

"Well, until about three. Dad went out to put flowers on Mother's grave."

So that was up in the air. Varallo didn't really think Lonnie had stabbed Rhoda Endicott; but on one like this, any deduction was in the wild blue yonder, you didn't have any way of guessing, and if you were lucky, you stumbled on X by chance. Whoever had used those scissors hadn't come there to do that; all experience, everything at the scene, said that X had just lost temper and control, probably for no longer than it took to kill the woman. It could have been Lonnie. It could have been one of the good Christians. And it could have been, and most probably had been, the casual breaker-inner panicked at finding someone at home.

Varallo had another sudden thought on that. No car. Endicott didn't own a car, and the little single garage had been open. The casual breaker-inner picking the place for that reason, assuming the house was empty? It was a million to one they'd ever pick up anybody for it, unless somebody had those prints on file.

———◆———

"I'm not surprised," said Mrs. Woods. "All I can say. The way she carried on. Scandalous. I said to my husband, if we still had the children at home we'd move out. But thank God they're both married and gone, because no denying it's a nice apartment and we couldn't get as cheap rent anywhere else around here."

Brenda Leeds, upstairs, had opened the door a crack and said crossly they weren't up yet, could they come back later, so O'Connor and Delia had been talking to neighbors. Mrs. Woods was the second one they'd tried; a deaf old lady named Sprague, across the hall from the Leeds', had said she didn't know anybody here, had just moved in.

"Why was that, Mrs. Woods?"

She was eyeing Delia interestedly. "I didn't know you had any policewomen in the department here. I can't say it's a job as I'd want a daughter of mine doing. Why, the way those women carried on, is what I meant. Those Leeds. The girl, she's in and out with a different boyfriend for every day of the week, and the mother just as bad. She'd have men up there, different men, nearly every afternoon, when the husband was off to work. Naturally, I couldn't tell you who they were, but I'd see them come and go—brazen as can be they were about it. You ask me, she was just begging to get herself murdered, picked up some nut, probably, at a bar or someplace. Maybe now the other two'll move out, you never know. I sure hope so. It's not very nice, having people like that in the same building."

"Well, isn't that interesting," said O'Connor when she'd shut the door. "Let's go back upstairs and ask Mr. Leeds if he knew anything about it." He was considerably annoyed when Brenda, now attired in a black sheath and spike-heeled pumps, told him that Daddy had gone to work.

"He had to. He's got the key of the store. He just went to open up and call Mr. Ring, he's the owner. He said to tell you he'd be right back. You needn't think—I mean, he feels just as bad as I do. But I don't know how we could tell you anything about what happened to Mother."

"Right back, hell," said O'Connor. "Where is he?"

"The C and M liquor store on Glenoaks," said the girl a little sullenly.

"Suppose you ask the lady some questions," said O'Connor to Delia, "while I get Mr. Leeds into the station for a little chat."

"We don't know anything about it," she said to his broad back. "Well, what do you want to ask? I don't think it's right, intruding on people when they've just lost a person—it was an awful shock, seeing her like that—I just couldn't stop shaking—"

"Yes, I'm sure it was." Delia could read this one at a glance: shallow but shrewd, probably quite amoral. The soothing syrup was not required; elementary deduction might have some shock value. "You work for the phone company, Miss Leeds? They work you some odd split shifts, don't they? So you'll be off some afternoons? Oh, most afternoons? Were you often at home here then?"

"Sometimes. Why?"

"Well, if you were here sometimes, possibly you can tell us about some of your mother's men friends? Who came here to see her when your father was at work?"

Brenda's vapid little mouth opened in shock, but it was the shock of surprise at a new idea. "But, for gosh sake," she said, "none of them would have done an awful thing like that! They all loved her—what else?"

"All?" said Delia. Human nature, human nature.

"Why, sure. Oh, gosh, I don't know who all of them were. Naturally, if she was expecting somebody up, I'd clear out, like with another girl in an apartment. You know." Brenda regarded Delia in her neat navy pantsuit a little doubtfully, and added with devastating frankness, "Or maybe you wouldn't. Anyway, I did. I don't know if I ought to tell you any of the ones I know. I didn't know them all, anyway. I think she found a new guy just last week."

For once, Delia was at a loss for a phrase. "You didn't think there was—er—anything wrong about it?"

"What's wrong?" said Brenda blankly. "You got to get what fun you can out of life, only live once, like they say. You do your thing, just so long as you're not hurting anybody else. Listen, like they say, variety's the spice of life. I got maybe four or five guys I make it with all the time, it's no skin off anybody's nose. I thought it was great Mother was still a real swinger."

"Well, it's very possible that one of those men did kill her," said Delia. "Do you know if she was in the habit of picking men up somewhere? Bars, or—"

"Oh gosh, I guess maybe," said Brenda. "I think that's how she met Johnny."

"Johnny." Delia got out her notebook.

"Gosh, I don't think he'd want me to tell you his name. Mother said he's got a real bitch of a wife, but she's got some money. Well, it's Jerome."

"Any others you know?"

"Gosh, it's awful to think it might've been like that—Mother so innocent, just picking up some guy and him turning out to be— Well, Steve Ashworth. And Max Reinhart. I don't know where any of them live. That's all I know."

Join the force and see life, thought Delia.

Delia had driven her own car here. Getting into it, she adjusted the rear-view mirror for the tenth time that morning—it needed tightening—and being offered a view of her own face, smiled at it. No, she wouldn't know how it was. There wasn't anything wrong with Delia Riordan's neat features; if she put on a wig and the green eye-shadow and sultry lipstick, doubtless a lot of people would think it was an improvement. Only of course in this job that you couldn't do. And it had to be this job.

Which was fine. A job she enjoyed, and was good at.

And now, after Brenda, she was going to see a pair of females probably as opposite as you could get. Or was she?

———◆———

They faced her there in the vice principal's office at Glendale High School. Ann Lane and Carol Beck, and they were scared, defiant, and defensive. They were both sixteen; Carol was the blond one, and prettier than Ann. And Delia heard a lot more from them than any of the men would have.

"They just don't understand!" said Carol. "It's the twentieth century, I mean! Look, some of the other girls at school go to church, but they're—they're *reasonable* kinds of churches. Not like the Word of God. I mean, they're not dead set against everything—against anybody having any fun—"

"And dating," said Ann. "Honestly, it isn't fair, every other girl our age dates regular, but the way our parents act, think we were little kids or something, it makes us look silly—can't date a guy till they meet him, like passing judgment or something, and only Friday nights because of studying the Bible lesson for church Saturday nights, and be home by eleven, and having to know where we're going—it's not fair when all the other girls—"

Delia was brisk on questions. "I'd have *died*," said Carol passionately. "I'd just have *died*, have Mike know about all that." Mike was Mike Rudd, a senior, a real swinger on campus, big man. Any girl'd be thrilled, Mike ask for a date, and he sort of played the field. "I nearly fainted when he asked me—and I'd have *died*, have to tell him my mother and father had to meet him before— And it was to

that movie they said was so awful, they'd *never* have let—he'd have
thought I was a real *nothing*, just a little *kid*—"

So they had told the Becks that Carol was going to stay over with
Ann—"like when we do our homework together—" "And see," said
Ann, "my room's got a sliding glass door from the patio and Mother
and Daddy's room's on the other side of the house. It was easy—I
knew it would be. Mike met Carol up at the corner like she told
him, and let her off here, it was way late, and she came around and
I let her in. We set the alarm and she got up at five-thirty, it was
still dark, and went up to the bus stop on Chevy Chase and waited
till I came and we just got the bus to the Becks' house, nobody ever
suspected—"

"And we figured nobody ever would, because Mother's been sort
of annoyed at Ann's mother ever since she wouldn't give her that
silly old family recipe for pecan pie—but then—"

"It was a lot of trouble to go to," said Delia.

"But it was *Mike Rudd!*" they said together, reverently. And suddenly Carol burst out crying and came out with some revealing inco-
herencies. "That awful old woman—just two days later, and we were
t-talking in the rest room at church—and her saying—it was just terrible, what she said to the poor black man, if you're going to *be* a
Christian, like Daddy's always saying—it was like the whited sepulchers in the Bible—and it was awful, but I said she was a hypocrite
and so did Ann, and she said—she said—and everybody sort of
pouncing on us— And, oh, Annie, it was *awful!* I didn't tell you—I
was ashamed, I pretended—it'd been great—but it was *awful!*" Carol
collapsed on the bench along one wall.

Delia offered Kleenex and a paper cup of water from the dis-
penser. Ann stared wide-eyed, and Carol gulped and sniffled and
mopped her eyes; she wouldn't look at either of them. "I said—it
was real great, but it wasn't—he—he tried to—he kept putting his
hands—and he made me drink some vodka—and the movie—just
awful things— And now all *this*, with us not allowed to go *anywhere*
and our allowances cut off and Daddy talking about serpents' teeth—
And I just *died*, Daddy coming to *school* and seeing Mike, and
Mike telling everybody—laughing, but he was mad—saying old fruit-

cake spout religion at him and I'm a real dog anyway— I don't *care*, I wouldn't go with him again, but everybody *knowing*—"

Delia patted the heaving shoulders absently and thought she'd like to meet Mike. Well, what Varallo said—on one like this, it was really all up in the air. Anything could have triggered the rage, the snatch at the convenient weapon.

But Delia was still thinking about that girl.

O'Connor was annoyed at Dudley Leeds before he saw him. He had chased down to that liquor store to find Leeds gone and the owner there. The owner didn't know where Leeds was; said he'd been there and gone. It was a damned shame about his wife. He was a reliable employee, sure, very steady, a nice guy. Worked there eight years.

O'Connor went back to the apartment; both Delia and the Leeds girl were gone.

Swearing, he went back to the office. Poor and Katz were in, Katz typing a report on the burglary. A slick job, said Poor, a lot of loot. A couple named Merwin, getting home late from a party, going straight to bed, never discovering the burglary till this morning. "It's funny how careless people will be. The good locks on the front and back doors, and a side door with a great big pane of glass in it. He never tried to fiddle the locks, just smashed the glass and went in. They gave us quite a list—a lot of good jewelry, tape recorders, couple of fur coats."

"People," said O'Connor, and went out for an early lunch. When he got back, everybody was there. Varallo had gotten back first, to take the dairy store clerk to look at mug shots, and he had made Daniel Ricketts. Now they just had to pick him up, whereupon the court would probably hand him thirty days and probation. There was another APB out on another heist man, William Maggott. Delia was talking seriously to Varallo, back at his desk. She gave O'Connor the gist of her interview with Brenda.

At one-twenty, Sergeant Duff called up and said a Mr. Leeds was here. O'Connor said, "Send him up!" and sat back in his chair, lighting another cigarette from the stub of his last one.

The man who came in a moment later was tall and slender, well-dressed in matching gray sports shirt and slacks. He hesitated in the door, and O'Connor beckoned him in. "Over here, Mr. Leeds."

Varallo came over to sit in. Leeds sat down in the indicated chair. He was lantern-jawed, tight-mouthed, with wary eyes. He said, "Brenda said you wanted to talk to me. Sorry, but I got responsibilities— I always open the store. This is the hell of a thing, about Wilma. Just the hell of a thing."

O'Connor was not disposed to use much tact here. He said brusquely, "Mr. Leeds, we'd like to know where you were last evening." Pending the autopsy, the woman had probably been killed last night.

"I don't know anything about what happened," said Leeds. "I was out."

"Where?"

"Down at Damon's bar. With a couple of pals. I was there from about six, I guess—there was a replay of the Rams' last game on TV. It ended about ten-thirty, and that's when I went home, and, my God, find cops all over the place, and Wilma—"

"Mr. Leeds," said O'Connor, "we have evidence that your wife had a number of lovers she entertained in your absence. Did you know anything about that?" He waited expectantly for the outburst.

"What?" said Leeds. "Well, sure. Sure she did. I got to say, it was quite a thing, woman her age still get the guys. She was forty-four, but you'd never know it. She picked up guys a lot younger, you had to hand it to her. She was quite a gal, Wilma."

O'Connor just looked at him, temporarily speechless. Varallo and Delia exchanged a look. O'Connor was, of course, despite outward appearances, the absolute puritan.

CHAPTER 5

Leeds supplied the names of the three pals with him at Damon's, and O'Connor went to see if he could find them. He tried the nearest one first, a Lee Davies up on Sonora Avenue. Davies turned out to be a Marine pensioner living with a married daughter, and he confirmed that Leeds had been with him and a couple of other guys at Damon's Monday night from about six on.

"Why? Cops asking about Dudley— you don't think he did anything? That's crazy. Anyway, he was there—the bartender could say so too, he knows all of us, we mostly go there, it's a nice place, nice people, friendly. What in hell you asking about Dudley for?"

O'Connor decided he'd let Dudley pass on the news about Wilma. Probably the bartender wouldn't come on duty until six or so; let the night watch check with him. He headed back down Sonora, and at the intersection of West Glenoaks came on a monumental mess. There were five cars involved, two of them reduced to rubble, two ambulances and four black-and-whites. He stopped to find out if it was going to turn into a felony for the detective office—all they needed—and Patrolman Murdock came up looking sick.

"Did you ever see such a mess, Lieutenant? Five dead, one of them a baby, my God. No, it won't be anything for you. We've got half a dozen eyewitnesses, and probably the doctor'll say he was drunk. The guy in the Pontiac. Came barreling down Glenoaks like a bat out of hell, doing about eighty per, never even hesitated for the light, and hit the Buick like a bomb, Buick minding its own business crossing on the green. The other cars were on the opposite side, sitting at the light. Nobody else really hurt, just shaken up, but everybody in the Buick—God. The Pontiac was registered to a Ronald Dunn. If it was him driving it, you won't be arresting him. He's practically in two pieces, went through the windshield and cut his throat."

"And no loss," said O'Connor. He went on back to the office. Delia came upstairs behind him and began to tell Varallo about the schoolgirls and Mike Rudd. "Tempest in a teapot," said Varallo.

"I talked to him," said Delia. "He was annoyed, you could say. He's big and arrogant and good-looking and thinks he's tough. You never know what a punk like that might do."

Burt came in and handed a manila envelope to O'Connor. "The photos on Leeds. We just got the kickback from the FBI on those prints from the Endicott place. Nobody knows them."

"So that's that." Varallo sat back and lit a cigarette. "Of course, nothing says they belong to X—anybody could have left them. I suppose the young pastor and his family had visitors occasionally."

"And I picked up three dandy clean latents on those glass fragments from the burglary this morning. Not in our files, I sent them to LAPD and the FBI, and I just had a buzz from LA. They made them; they're sending over his package."

"Well, a step in the right direction," said O'Connor. He upended the envelope over his desk and started to look at the glossy eight-by-tens.

"I don't think we'll give you anything on Leeds at all. You can see by the photos, the place was a mess. Looked as if it hadn't been cleaned up in weeks. We picked up a million smudges and some pretty clear prints—both the other Leeds kicked up a fuss over having their prints taken—but most of 'em belong to the corpse and them, and the few that don't could be irrelevant. There was a lot of stuff all around that room, but it didn't look to me as if any of it could say anything about the homicide."

"The lover boys," said O'Connor. "And if it was one of them, every reason his prints would be there."

"What it comes to," said Varallo to Delia, "we've poked around at the possible personal angle on it, and not much has shown. So we get back to basics and do some routine legwork on it." He looked at his watch. "Day after tomorrow. Day off be damned, I've got to get all those roses wrapped up. Coldest winter in forty years, they say. I never knew it to go below freezing before."

"You should complain, with what the East's going through." O'Connor leafed through the photos distastefully. "Bunch of god-damned riffraff. Woman old enough to know better picking up men in bars. Asking to get beaten up."

"You're just a puritan, Charles," grinned Varallo. "How many times do we see it? I'm taking off early— I've got to pick up all that burlap."

O'Connor took off a little early too. When he turned into the drive of the house on Virginia Avenue, Katharine had the outside lights on for him. He laid a hand on the gate, braced himself firmly, went in, and was staggered back by some hundred pounds of affectionate dog. "Down, girl!" Maisie now had her full growth at nearly two years of age, and was outsize even for an Afghan hound. And what with one thing and another, he never had gotten her into obedience training. She had a good loud bark as a watchdog, if she loved everybody, but the only other benefit he had from his blue girl, even as Katharine had predicted, was that he got a lot of exercise running after her on the weekly excursion up into the hills.

She pushed rudely past him into the kitchen, and Katharine said, "You're early."

"I get fed up with this job." He kissed her soundly. "Stop fussing over a hot stove and have a civilized drink with me before dinner."

"No fussing, it's all in the oven. Fine with me."

They carried the drinks down to look in on the baby. "Now, he sleeps," said O'Connor. Young Vincent Charles, with a full stomach, lay placidly in peaceful slumber in the antique cradle Katharine had refinished.

"Like a lamb," she said fondly. She didn't sound so fond some seven hours later when she sat up in bed, switched on the lamp, and said crossly, "I'm coming!" as she felt for slippers and robe. The time bomb had gone off.

O'Connor swore and turned over, but a minute later Maisie started. Either she was imitating the baby or trying to outyell him. Her voice rose in an unearthly howl from the living room, and Katharine said, "Damn!"

"Don't put her out, for God's sake," said O'Connor over the din. "We'll have the neighbors down on us."

"Look, I can sleep days," said Katharine. "You shut the door and try to ignore us, darling."

O'Connor put the pillow over his head, but he didn't get back to sleep for a couple of hours. When he woke up at seven, everybody else was dead to the world—Katharine beside him, the baby in the cradle, Maisie snoring on the living-room couch after a hard night.

"Why anybody deliberately chooses to go through this—" said O'Connor to himself. He shaved and dressed and went out to Pike's on Glenoaks for breakfast.

It was Varallo's day off, also Delia's. Katz came in as O'Connor sat down at his desk, Forbes and Poor immediately after. Forbes said he felt better. He wasn't coughing so much.

The package had come up from LAPD on the burglar. O'Connor had a rapid look at the night report—nothing, common assault at a bar, another hit-and-run—and opened that up. The burglar was Andrew Calloway, black, 32, 190, black and brown; he had quite a little record, mostly of burglary, going back seven years. His last known address was Pasadena. O'Connor tossed the envelope over to Poor. "So go see if he's there."

Katz had gotten buzzed by the desk and was on the phone, frowning. When he put the phone down he said to nobody in particular, "That's funny," and went out.

Poor tucked the record on Calloway into his breast pocket and followed him, and O'Connor reached for the phone with a sigh, opening the top drawer of his desk. Burt had handed him an address book from the Leeds' apartment, evidently Wilma's, and it had a few addresses in it but more anonymous phone numbers labeled with first names. The lover boys.

Wesley had gone to work yesterday, but today he had to make the funeral arrangements; they had notified him that the body would be released. Such a queer way to put it. He worried about the money again. He said, "Forest Lawn would be too expensive. I ought to conduct the— I couldn't, not—not for Mother. I don't know what to do, about money. I couldn't ask for an advance on my salary. And there's the will, I'll have to go to a lawyer to do something about that, and he'd want money too."

Eileen had hardly heard him, hardly noticed him leave. But aware of his anxious tone, she thought as she combed her hair, rummaged for the stub of a lipstick, that you'd never have thought he'd be clever enough to trick her. And of course in a way he hadn't: She had just been so stupid.

It had been a queer engagement, not like Danny. He had seldom kissed her, held her; when he did, it was reluctant, brief. He had said the right things as if dutifully, love you, my dear, so happy. But nobody else was like Danny, and Wesley was shy. She hadn't especially wanted him to kiss her. She was numb all over again, that time, for Mother Ruth's dying.

They were married two weeks after Mother Ruth died, and they didn't go anywhere on a trip; they just came down here to Wesley's new church, the three of them, because he said there wasn't much money. And of course it wasn't bells ringing and lightning going off, the way it was supposed to be, the way it would have been with Danny. It wasn't anything, just awkward and clumsy and uncomfortable. She knew right away he didn't know how to love anybody that way, it didn't mean anything to him. It was nearly as if he had to force himself to touch her.

The old woman, so near in the little house?

But the very week they came here, she found out why. The church and the house had been dirty, not properly cleaned in years. The old pastor, just dead, had been a widower, lived here alone. Eileen had been washing the church windows that day, rather enjoying seeing the grime come off, the sparkle on the clean glass. She'd gone back to the house for more rags, and the door had been open; they hadn't heard her coming.

"—Quite pleased with the girl, Wesley? She seems like a nice, lady-like girl."

"Yes, of course." His voice had been evasive, but the old woman seemed not to notice.

"Mrs. Kruger trained her well, she's quite a good little housekeeper. As long as you had to get married—"

"I must say, I still think it's very high-handed," he burst out, "that the deacons should have the right to—to dictate like that. Nobody ever told me they have that rule, all pastors have to be married before having a church."

"I expect they've found it saves trouble. I can remember Grandfather talking about foolish women taking notions to the minister."

"Well, it's very high-handed. Telling people what to do."

Why hadn't she gone in right then, said, So that's why, said, You don't really want me, said—? At least, however poor a little substitute, she had thought Wesley offered her the love and security she had lost; then she found he offered her nothing, and she was lost again and abandoned.

The English lit teacher at high school, Mrs. Sayers, had been a great admirer of the Victorian poets. If ever she assigned you something to memorize, it was bound to be Tennyson or Shelley or Swinburne. There was a line of Tennyson's that came unbidden into Eileen's mind, once, about that time and how she'd reacted to it: *I embrace the purpose of God and the doom assigned.* Maybe she had started to live by that, never realizing it.

She had said and done nothing. Nothing to Wesley when he never again came to her bed. The hurt of knowing she wasn't loved or wanted started the ice numbing her all over again, and that was the time she had turned to the books and pictures for any real life of her own. That was safe. She could forget them both for hours at a time; she would walk up to the beautiful new library, browse among the books for hours, all day sometimes, sitting there to read, or outside in the shade in the lovely grounds. Or walk up to Forest Lawn.

He was away all day, at his job. She had been surprised that the church didn't pay him enough to live on. And Mrs. Endicott was supposed to be rich. But she had a deep, miserly streak; that check coming every month, mostly just to be deposited in the bank. At least that was how it had been since Wesley had to take it to the bank for her. He owed her all the cost of divinity school, she said. She would ask him to get money, write little checks, for the small treats for herself—the chocolate fudge, the special tea.

All that time, Eileen paid as little notice as possible to them. Lost herself in the books, the pictures. When you were deep in a book you couldn't feel unhappy in yourself; it was only after you closed it that you came back to being yourself and remembered.

Now, looking back clearly, she saw how stupid that had been, too. If this had happened then, she'd have had no defenses at all. But it hadn't, it couldn't have, of course, because it hadn't been the time.

Now she had been calm and cool, with some newfound hardness and control, to answer the policewoman's questions quite sensibly and logically. The police hadn't come back again. It was going to be all right.

Pay for what you did wrong. But she really didn't see why she should have to suffer a long time, perhaps, for something that hadn't taken a minute to do, just because she'd been stupid for three years. And now there was a queer idea in her mind about it. Suppose she had paid already?

Coming out of the slough of despond she'd been in, she thought how she had hated the old woman, all the things she had had to do for her, the old woman accepting ungraciously, demanding. If it had been Mother Ruth, she'd have done it all in love and tenderness. But the old woman whose God was a petty tyrant, whose very love for Wesley was selfish and dominating, the only love she knew— The ugly, sagging old flesh to wash, lift, help onto the toilet, into the tub, dress and undress— It was queer to think, maybe she'd paid the penance before she did the wrong.

Time—in some of those books about astral travel and telepathy and all the rest—speculations about time. She hadn't understood the Dunne man at all, but it seemed that time wasn't what everyone thought it was. *The doom assigned.* Maybe it had all been fated, she'd had no choice at all, either to marry Wesley, or go, or stay. Because all those years, the Dream had predicted it, had forecast it all. It had all been fixed in time ahead.

If she had already paid, that should end it. If she had still to pay, she would accept that for another life, another time.

Wesley came home in late afternoon and told her about the funeral. "They were very nice. It seems to be all right, they take something down and you can pay later. I explained about the will. And I found a lawyer in the phone book."

She wasn't interested. He said, "I haven't got a sermon for Sunday." But he didn't make any move to start writing one; he kept staring at her, and he couldn't keep an awful speculation from his eyes. "You look different. You've got on—a lot of makeup."

"Not a lot. A new lipstick. I paid a dollar and a half for it at the market." It slid into her mind, how he had had to do all the marketing, at the big Safeway three blocks down Central, and how he had always looked embarrassed when she put Kotex down on the list. He didn't like or understand women, or want to, or know that that was unnatural. "I am different," she said dreamily. "I feel different. Maybe it's just that I'm catching up on all the sleep I missed. I've been so tired—so tired, for two whole years. Walking around in a dream."

There was fear in his eyes again. "I'd better—the sermon," he muttered. "Be up late—not disturb you."

He didn't come to their room at all; he slept in the old woman's room.

Wednesday was one of those days where they got out and around, with variable results. Poor had gone off hunting Calloway, and Katz hadn't come back from wherever he'd gone when the LAPD station in North Hollywood called. The APB had finally turned up Daniel Ricketts, just picked up out there. Forbes went to ferry him in, and O'Connor talked to the phone company. He could have gone out to look at the couple of lover boys who had addresses appended, but he'd have to sit in on questioning Ricketts.

That didn't take long. He wasn't very bright, but when they explained to him that two of his victims had picked out his mug shot, he saw it was a waste of time saying he hadn't done anything. O'Connor called in a request for a warrant, and Forbes took him over to the jail to book him in. Katz came back talking to himself; he didn't seem interested in talking to anybody else, and sat brooding over a city map before beginning to type a report. They were shorthanded, with two detectives off.

O'Connor spent most of the day, unproductively, on the Leeds thing. He got six of the unlabeled numbers identified by the phone company by ten o'clock, and left them to work on the rest; those and the other names in the address book would occupy him to end of his shift. He spent the day driving—Eagle Rock, Pasadena, La Cañada, into LA—looking for and at the lover boys, and he didn't get one single damned useful thing.

Most of those he talked to were casual about it. None of them were bums, but ordinary working men in ordinary jobs, a couple in their thirties, most older, most unmarried, divorced, or whatever. Sure, they'd known Wilma, great gal, Wilma. It had been very much the casual thing. A couple of them hadn't known she was married. The only one who acted nervous was John Jerome, and he had a reason: the wife with a little money. He was a mechanic at a garage in Glendale; he'd met Wilma about six months ago, when she brought her car in. "I hope to God this don't all have to come out, Lieutenant."

"When did you see her last?"

"Uh—last Saturday. Afternoon. The wife and kids went to a show. Listen, I wouldn't have done anything to Wilma!" He had an alibi, anyway; he'd been at home Monday night with his family.

O'Connor didn't think they'd nab anybody for Wilma. Those photos—in his experience, when there wasn't much physical evidence at the scene, that was one that ended up in Pending, because you hadn't any handle. The Endicott thing was another example, just no physical evidence at the scene, and they might as well forget about it right now; but if he knew Vic, he'd work it into the ground.

Wilma, of course, had been no great loss, but it annoyed O'Connor to be stymied this way. He'd wasted practically the whole day. Whoever had beaten the woman to death—at least, that was what it had looked like—wasn't necessarily listed in the address book, but that was one hard fact of life in detective work: the routine has to be done.

He got back to the office at four-thirty to see what had been going on. Katz told him that Poor and Forbes had wasted practically the whole day, looking for that burglar Calloway. "He'd moved from the address LA had, but he'd left a forwarding address—don't laugh, he gets a regular disability pension from the Navy—and it was in

Pacoima. So they went out there—John called in, said the traffic was murder—and found it was his married sister's place. He'd moved again, and is now living with a pal some place in Montrose or La Crescenta, she thinks, and the place is rented by the pal. She can't think of the pal's name, but Calloway used to work with him at a bowling alley in Eagle Rock. So John and Jeff chased down there to look at the alley's employment records, and finally found the names of three men who worked there when Calloway did. The last time John called, he thought they'd pinned it down, but that was nearly an hour ago."

"Why anybody wants to be a cop—" said O'Connor sourly. He looked at his unnaturally neat desk, sat down, and picked up the phone. "Get me Goulding, Al."

He waited some time for him, and when Goulding finally answered he said, "I sort of expected an autopsy report on Leeds today."

"Oh you did?" said Goulding. "You haven't visited the morgue lately, have you? That crash yesterday—five DOA's, and about the messiest ones you ever saw. I'd done the Leeds autopsy, but I haven't got the report done—I'll get to it, don't rush me. I'd like to get these bodies all inventoried and out of here and the place cleaned up as soon as possible. I'd also like to know what the insurance company'll end up paying out—the driver of the car that bombed the second one was full to the gills, I'm surprised he was still conscious. In fact, of course he may have passed out at the wheel. But it still surprises me occasionally to see just how much mayhem a high-speed crash can inflict on the human body."

"Well, I'd appreciate a report on Leeds sometime," said O'Connor.

Just as he put down the phone, Poor and Forbes came in with a tall, light-skinned black. They looked tired, and Forbes was coughing again.

"Well, congratulations," said Katz. "It was a tough fight, but you made it."

"Talk about bloodhounding, just the word for it," said Poor.

"I told you I haven't done nothing," said Calloway.

"Yes, you did," said Forbes. "Several times. We happen to know different."

O'Connor and Katz took pity on them and did the talking to him, in an interrogation room down the hall. He went on saying he hadn't done anything, and they explained to him about the fingerprints, and finally he said, "Oh, hell. I never thought about that glass. You guys sure do look close at everything, don't you?" He sounded aggrieved.

"So where's the loot?" asked O'Connor.

But that he wouldn't say. A description of the loot had been added to the hot list for all pawnbrokers; but Calloway was a pro and would use a pro fence, or several fences. He knew he wouldn't get much time; he might be out in a year or less, and he wouldn't give away his fences. The loot was long gone, little hope of ever turning it up; the jewelry would have been broken up by now.

"The Merwins can just put it down to experience," said Poor, yawning. "I gave them a little lecture about security—I bet they take it to heart." Katz took Calloway over to book him in.

O'Connor, tired and aware that he'd wasted the day, drove home, and Maisie knocked the breath out of him against the driveway gate. He went in and told Katharine he needed a drink. She was holding the baby— "He's been fussing a little, maybe he's starting to teethe early"—and O'Connor regarded his robust young son with a reluctant grin.

"Little devil." He prodded the baby's stomach softly and provoked a gargantuan belch. "Going to keep us awake all night again?"

"You know something?" said Katharine. "I'll bet you were just as bad, Charles."

———◆———

On Thursday morning, with Katz off and O'Connor roping Poor and Forbes in on the Leeds thing, Varallo said to Delia, "So let's do a little routine. That's one grim fact you'll learn about the thankless job—there's always the slogging routine to do."

"Oh, I know about that," said Delia. "Did you get your roses all wrapped up?"

He looked to see if she was laughing at him, but she looked merely interested. "Silly sort of hobby to get involved in—for a cop, isn't it?

They were there when we bought the house, and I just—well, got interested. Yes, I got them all covered, so now I suppose it'll turn
warmer."

They went down to Records together, and commandeered Burt
and Thomsen to help. They didn't have any computers yet, and
while everything was crossfiled, it would be a little job. What they
were looking for were the names of men who'd been picked up for
the daylight burglaries; there wouldn't be too many of those, but ten
times more than there would have been say, five years ago. That kind
of casual crime had soared.

By eleven o'clock they had sorted out eleven men who might be
possibles for Rhoda Endicott. That wasn't all there were, just the
ones Varallo liked best. Only one of them had only one count, of B
and E during daylight hours; the rest had varying records, three, five,
six counts, some night burglaries, but they had all been dropped on
in daylight too.

"And just to break one more fact of life to you," said Varallo, "we
can find them all and question them, but it's a thousand to one we'll
ever arrest anybody for it. There's no physical evidence."

"Why do we do it?" asked Delia obediently. "As if I didn't
know."

"Because sometimes, just like the Bible says, the wicked flee where
no man pursueth. Lean on one of these characters, we know you
done it, brother, tell us all, just occasionally one of them comes
apart. And then of course if you haven't got a witness, or didn't spell
out all his rights, the court throws it out. It's far more likely," said
Varallo seriously, "that we'll come across one we're morally sure did
it, and never be able to pin it on him. Or we may not. Anyway, let's
do it."

The addresses were all in the area, but that took in quite a little
territory, the Glendale annex up above La Crescenta, Montrose, La
Crescenta itself. They took the Mercedes in case they decided to
bring one of them in. "It'd save time if we split up," said Delia.

"No dice. Some of these characters are big and strong."

She looked at him soberly, getting out her keys. "You know, Vic, I
do understand the job. I know some judo. I never thought it was a
glamorous job."

It was the first time she'd used his name. He smiled at her. "I know. It's just, we don't tend to—um—think of you as equals, lady. Just superiors, to be looked after."

Delia laughed. "And most of us like it just that way. Only with me, after hours." They got in the car.

"This is quite a vintage baby. They go on forever, of course. You had it long?"

"Oh yes. It was," said Delia rather flatly, "my father's."

They had a busy day. They found five of the men to talk to. The ones who interested Varallo the most were Peter Santori and Esteban Garcia. Santori had committed three known daylight break-ins; Garcia, four. Since you could usually postulate a dozen or so crimes for every one that ended in arrest, that gave both of them a good deal of probable experience. Garcia had also been charged, six months ago, with a knifing.

Neither of them had any produceable alibi. Santori said, after thinking about it, that he'd been at home all day Sunday. Home was a single room in an old hotel on South Central. It had a nomadic population, and the desk clerk didn't take much notice of comings or goings; he couldn't back up Santori. Garcia was even more nebulous. He lived with a good-sized family of parents, brothers, and sisters, an old aunt and an older grandmother, in a ramshackle rented house down by the SP tracks. He had an old VW. Santori didn't have a car. Santori was on welfare; Garcia had a part-time job with a maintenance gardening service. He said he'd been out on Sunday, just driving around seeing some guys.

They both acted very nervous of cops.

"I like them both," said Varallo in the car. "I like Santori better. Tell me why."

"The car and the map," said Delia.

"That's my smart little detective. Santori hasn't got a car. If he was out roaming around looking for a likely place to loot, well, he wasn't far from the Endicott place to start with. It'd be about four blocks down from that hotel. Garcia was farther away, call it a mile or so, but he's got a car."

"I thought Santori reacted when you mentioned Elm Street."

"So did I. Pay your money and take your choice. Burglars per se tend to be rather jumpy, nervous fellows. Entering a supposedly empty house—possibly spotting it as empty because of no car in the gargage—"

"Yes, I thought of that too."

"—And being confronted by an old lady, either scared or angry, shouting at him, most burglars would just cut and run. Could we say, in other days? You can't separate violent crime from crime against property just so clearly as we used to do. Garcia jumped somebody with a knife before. Santori knocked one householder down and gave him a concussion getting away."

"Garcia," said Delia, "might habitually carry a knife."

"These hot-headed Latins. Yes. And so have been more likely to reach for it than a pair of scissors, even if they were in plain sight. And then again—think of where the wheelchair was."

"What about it?"

"Only just inside the living room, near that little hall. He wouldn't have expected the house to be unlocked; he'd slide around to the back door. It was open, so in he went. Not leaving those prints on the kitchen door—that could have been anybody visiting the Endicotts. He gets into the bedroom, where the scissors were on the bed, when the old lady hears him—she could move the chair, and—"

"Sorry, the scissors were on the bed in the front bedroom. Off the living room."

"*Per l'amore di Dio!*" said Varallo violently. "*Diavolo!* They were? Well, all right. She could get around the house in the chair, she was in the back bedroom. Her room. And he slid through into the living room, the front bedroom, looking for possible loot. Not noticing her. She wheels herself into the living room, maybe shouting at him, or shouting for help—he's trapped there, he snatches up the scissors and runs at her—and in getting past, in that narrow door, he half turns the wheelchair around."

"Very fine, full-blooded stuff," said Delia. "He certainly could have. Either one of them."

"So," said Varallo, "I think we let them both sit for a day or so. Go and look at the rest of these. And when they're both thinking we've accepted their tales, we'll haul them in to the station, to make it look more official, and lean on them again. Rather, let Charles.

That's one place, lady, nobody of your sex can ever compete. A big tough supermale cop like Charles comes in very useful at leaning on the suspects."

Delia burst out laughing, and she had a warm, infectious laugh. "I can believe that!"

They looked in at the office at the end of the shift and found O'Connor swearing about another wasted day. They'd been out talking to more of Wilma's lover boys, all for nothing. Just after Delia had gone out, and Varallo was about to leave, a call came in from Pasadena. The APB had turned up the other heist man, William Maggott. Would Glendale like to come get him?

"Hell and damnation!" said O'Connor. "Right at the end of the day!"

Forbes said resignedly he'd go over and get him, and stash him away for Rhys and Hunter to talk to.

On Friday morning. Varallo and Delia checked in at the office to see if anything new had gone down. Overnight, the usual drunks, an attempted knifing in a bar; nothing for the detectives. The Secret Service agent, Downs, charged in energetically and announced to O'Connor, "We got a damn good latent off that latest phony bill, by the ninhydrin process. It's on the wire to the FBI, but we want to check your records and LAPD."

"Be our guest."

Katz said to Varallo, "You getting anywhere on the minister's mother? I used to think I was a fairly smart detective. Well, something turns up to say your brilliant deductions are all wrong, you just start over."

"What?" said Varallo.

"These damn vandalisms. It worked out like clockwork, on paper," said Katz. "And very funny-peculiar too, every single one of them, new moon, full moon. Since August, for God's sake. Also, the same area—not a very big area—between Kenneth Road and Glenoaks, north and south, and Sonora and Highland, east and west. Not that it gave us anywhere to look or anybody to look at, but I thought at least we knew that much."

"So?" said Varallo.

"So, Wednesday morning we get another. If I'm right, it's not time for another one. And it's way out of the area—down on Carlton Street off Chevy Chase. But looking part of the same picture, car in unlocked garage, air let out of the tires, windshield smashed. I guess I've been woolgathering," said Katz. "Lane was annoyed as hell, and you can't blame—"

"Lane?" said Delia quickly.

"Carl Lane. The owner. He—"

"Oh really," said Delia. She looked at Varallo. "The routine—it usually pays off, I know. But once in a while a detective has a hunch too. And right now I've got a hunch. I think I'd like to follow it up."

"Just on malicious mischief?"

CHAPTER 6

"Oh," said Mike Rudd. "You're back, the lady cop. Who's the movie star?"

"Detective Varallo," said Delia crisply. "You were really teed off about the lecture you got from Carol's father, weren't you? How come you waited over a week to get back at him?"

He stared at them, taken aback at the sudden challenge. He was a big, good-looking kid with wavy brown hair to his shoulders, an athlete's hard body. "What the hell," he said. "What do you mean?"

"Don't act any stupider than you are," said Delia. "You were mad about it. You thought that was where Carol lived, because you'd dropped her off there, after your date. And then you got the lecture from Beck, leading his daughter astray. You got back at him, maybe on impulse, Tuesday night. Did a little damage to his car."

"You can't prove that."

"Would you like to see us try?" said Varallo. "You just made a little mistake, Mike—you got somebody else's wheels."

"You don't scare me, cop! You can't come down on me for anything, I won't be eighteen till June. You can't print me." How quickly they learned that one. They'd gotten him out of class, sent to the vice principal's office; an impassive secretary sat out of hearing across the room.

Varallo said to Delia, "I don't know why we're wasting time here. These snot-nose kids playing silly games—this punk wouldn't have the guts even for a caper like that—"

"Goddamn it, I got more guts than you think—what the hell's the big deal? So I let the air out of his tires—that fruitcake, that Neanderthal, talking at me like I was a mad rapist or something—and bring *cops* down at me, for God's sake! So what do you do, put

me in jail and throw the key away? Try it. My mom's got a lawyer
for a boyfriend."

"Thanks so much. We just wanted to know," said Delia sweetly.
There wasn't, of course, much they could do to a juvenile. It was malicious mischief, a misdemeanor. Make it a formal charge, maybe a
month from now there'd be a hearing in juvenile court, probation. It
wasn't worth the time.

Incongruously, Rudd was more aggrieved to see them turn away.
"Hey. Hey, I said I did it—aren't you going to do something? I
figured that little creep snuck out to meet me, but I sure didn't
know she came out of the Ark, that old guy talking about God—
Hey."

"Do you feel like doing all the paperwork and spending a couple
of hours in juvenile court?" asked Varallo in the hall.

"No way. I just had the hunch. And I probably sparked it off, talking to him the other day," said Delia. "Just the random impulse to
do a little damage."

"At least he isn't cluttering up Joe's brilliant deductions any more.
Joe'll be pleased about that. So," said Varallo, "let's go look at some
more daylight burglars."

As Delia slid behind the wheel she said, "That list of church
members. We never really talked to any of them."

"I put that one on the back burner awhile. It was always likelier it
was the casual break-in. Of course, I will say, by what you heard
from Mrs. Clifford, most of the good Christians disapproved of Mrs.
Endicott's lack of brotherly love, and weren't feeling so loving toward her. If we don't hit pay dirt at the routine, we may go back and
look at some of them—but right now, I'm still liking Santori a lot.
Sometime we'll see if Charles can scare him more than I did."

———————————◆———————————

The funeral was at the mortuary, not the church. Eileen had only
been to two other funerals in her life, and this one was entirely
different. The mortuary was Kiefer and Eyrick's, near the library,
and there was a little chapel with the coffin on a stand, and some
flowers. Not many flowers.

She sat alone with Wesley in the family room, a gauze curtain be-

tween them and the public chapel; she couldn't see how many people had come. The mortuary had supplied a minister, but he didn't
say much; he hadn't known her, and Wesley probably wouldn't have
remembered to tell him much. Devoted wife and mother, he said.
He read some psalms. The organ swelled solemnly, and people filed
past the coffin. She and Wesley went last; she didn't want to look at
the old woman again, and averted her eyes.

The coffin in a long black car. She and Wesley in another. The
slow ride through town to the cemetery. It was an old cemetery, the
Grandview Cemetery, and she was glad, so very glad, that it wasn't
Forest Lawn. Forest Lawn too expensive.

The first time she'd seen it was just after they'd come here, one
Sunday. Mrs. Meecham, talking to them after church, had said she
was going to put flowers on her husband's grave, and would they like
to come? As newcomers to town—it was one of the landmarks. Harriet Meecham had driven them all around to see the Court of Lib-
erty, the Court of David, the great murals, and the stained glass in
the mausoleum. It was the most beautiful place Eileen had ever
seen. Afterward, she had gone there alone. The entrance, through
the tall iron gates, was only about ten blocks from the house. She
couldn't go up the hill to the churches, the other buildings, it was
too far without a car, but she often went just inside the great gates
to the expanse of cool lush green lawn, the white marble sculpture
where the fountain played and the graceful swans swam in a pond.

She was glad the old woman wasn't going to be there, even her old
shell. It would have spoiled the beauty a little.

Quite a few of the church people came to the cemetery, just as a
mark of respect. They came up to Wesley afterward and said trite
conventional things, and went away. The long black car took Wesley
and Eileen home to the little house. He had hardly spoken to her
since Wednesday, and after standing a few minutes in the middle of
the living room, looking around helplessly, he went into his mother's
room and shut the door.

"Well, for the love of sweet Christ!" said O'Connor disgustedly.
He had just come back from lunch. There had been a new heist

pulled at a liquor store on East Glenoaks just after it opened at ten, and Forbes and Poor were out on that; only Katz was there to look up enquiringly. "Damn Goulding and his messy bodies! Now we've got most of that to do over, for God's sake! We took it for granted—*and*, for Christ's sake, we all ought to know better—"

"What's up?" said Katz.

O'Connor slapped the autopsy report down in front of him. "Read it and weep!" It was, at last, the autopsy report on Wilma Leeds, and it contained a few surprises. She had died of a severe beating, said Goulding, putting it in correct technical terms: actual cause of death, a fractured skull. No evidence that she'd engaged in sexual relations within twelve hours of death. And she had died between four-thirty and five-thirty on Monday afternoon. "Well, that is a little surprise," said Katz, coming to that. "Whatever alibis you picked up for that evening don't mean a damn thing."

"And the husband was at work. Sweet *Christ!*" said O'Connor. "If I have to talk to all those men again—" Before he could do any more swearing, Poor and Forbes came in and tossed a quarter for who'd do the report.

"We got a good description from the clerk. He's downstairs looking at mug shots. Oh, Burt sent you a present—just came through on the telex." Forbes handed O'Connor a yellow sheet.

"Don't tell me we're going to get lucky." It was a kickback from the feds on one set of the strange prints in the Leeds' apartment. They belonged to William Dunninger, who had a little record of assault from four years back in Elgin, Illinois. "I've got him," said O'Connor, scrabbling among papers. "The phone company just turned him up. Come on, Joe, let's go talk to him. At least he sounds more possible than anybody else we've seen."

They found Dunninger without much trouble; the apartment manager knew where he worked, at a men's store on Wilshire. He was a lanky, balding man of about forty; he blinked at the badges and said, "What's up?"

They told him. "Well, what do you know!" said Dunninger. "That's real sad, about Wilma. Sure, I knew her pretty well. Well, I met her at a party at somebody's place, a while ago. Listen, you don't think I had anything to do with it?"

"You've got a count of assault back East," O'Connor reminded him.

"That? You got to be kidding. I was tanked up, and this guy called me a name, and I landed a few on him. Ten days and probation."

"So tell us where you were last Monday afternoon," invited Katz.

"Where the hell would I be? I was right here, waiting on customers," said Dunninger. "I got a job, haven't I? The last time I saw Wilma was about two weeks ago. Look, she was just an easy lay to me. What call would I have—"

"Anybody back up the alibi?" asked O'Connor.

"Sure, you think I'm alone in a place this size? The manager, Mr. Miner, and the other clerk, Al Hahn."

O'Connor looked at Katz. "Round and round the mulberry bush," he said. "Let's put it in Pending."

But being a fairly dogged cop, he wouldn't do that for a while.

Rhys was sitting on night watch alone; it was Hunter's night off. It was a slow night; nothing came in at all until nine-fifty, when he had a call from a squad car. A body found in a car, at Mountain and Ross.

He drove up there to look at it and found Patrolmen Tracy and Fenner, riding swing patrol, standing by. "It got reported by the householder coming home," said Tracy. "I don't think it's been here long. This isn't a main drag, but there'd be some traffic occasionally, and most people would report an accident."

"Yes, but was it?" said Rhys. The car was a white two-year-old Dodge. It was angled violently into the curb, one front wheel over the curb, headlights and motor still on. Most of the front end had gotten caught up against a tree, or it might have plowed right on down into the householder's front yard. Rhys peered in the driver's door, which was ajar; Tracy said it had been locked, he'd jimmied it open in case she needed first aid.

She didn't; she was dead; no pulse at all. In the light of the waning moon and his flashlight, Rhys could just see that she wasn't a young woman, if she didn't look elderly either. There didn't seem to be a mark on her, no blood, and no smell of liquor.

"Could have had a heart attack, I suppose. The doctor'll tell us. Any ID?"

"Not a smell, no handbag at all. The registration was in the glove compartment." Fenner handed it over. The Dodge was wearing Arizona plates and was registered to Richard Osborne at an address in Tucson.

"Well, it'll be for the day watch," said Rhys. "Nothing anybody can do tonight." He called the morgue and the garage. The wagon came for the body, and the garage towed the car in.

It was waiting on Saturday morning. The clerk at the liquor store had given a good description of the heist man, and Katz and Poor had finished yesterday in Records, pulling the packages on men who more or less matched the description. Now they had to find them and question them. The Leeds thing was still up in the air, and there were still some daylight burglars Varallo wanted to look at. At least everybody was in today.

O'Connor passed Rhys' report on to Delia. "You can get on this. Joe, it's just occurred to me that we haven't asked Wilma's neighbors the right questions. I'll bet most of those women used to gawk out the windows to see the lover boys come and go—women being women. When we assumed it'd been after dark, we didn't ask. Now I think we'd better."

Everybody went out, and Delia murmured to herself, "Some more equal than others. Just a glorified Girl Friday." But it was another job that had to be done.

She got on the phone to Tucson, got the number, asked for Richard Osborne, introduced herself, and explained. His voice went high and alarmed. "My mother's driving the Dodge—she's been staying with my sister in Hollywood. Oh my God, did you say *dead*? An accident? Oh my God, we'll come—you'd better get hold of Cindy—"

She got the name and address before he slammed the receiver down. She talked to Miss Cindy Osborne in Hollywood. "—Been just sick with worry when she didn't come home, she went to see an old friend in Glendale, she used to live there before Dad died and she went over to Dick's— I called the police, Mrs. Mills said she left just after nine—"

She got there half an hour later, a pretty girl in her twenties, and Delia took her over to the morgue, where she identified the body as her mother, Mrs. Edna Osborne. "But was it an accident? Oh my God—she was only fifty-seven—" But she was pretty well in control, and she asked then, "Why didn't anybody notify us when it happened? She carried identification— Oh. Oh." She put a hand to her temple. "I just remembered—when I called Mrs. Mills she said Mother'd forgotten her bag. She had the car keys in her pocket, and —but what was it, a stroke or—"

"The doctor will find out," said Delia. It had all the indications of a heart attack. It made some more paperwork; there was always enough of that to do.

Delia felt a little annoyed at the men, barging out on real business and leaving her to run the office. But Varallo had the list of daylight burglars. She sat down at her desk and lit a cigarette moodily and wondered if any of them were getting anywhere.

O'Connor and Katz had talked to Mr. and Mrs. Hartman in the apartment at the end of the hall from the Leeds', and Mr. and Mrs. Fisher in the left rear downstairs; on a Saturday, not everybody was home. Mrs. Hartman admitted that she'd looked out for the men coming to see Wilma. "Gave us all something to talk about, anyway. She was a hussy if I ever saw one." But Mrs. Hartman hadn't been home on Monday afternoon. "And we went out to a movie that night, missed all the excitement."

Mrs. Fisher, however, had been home. "Not that I'd demean myself to keep a deliberate watch on that slut," she said with a sniff, and immediately proceeded to show how she had, by giving them a description of the two men she'd seen going in there, one on Friday and one on Saturday. But there hadn't been anybody on Monday afternoon. Not a soul.

"And I'll bet she'd know if there had been," said Katz.

"No bets," said O'Connor. "She's at the rear of the building downstairs, and Wilma was upstairs in front. Fisher wouldn't be lurking in the hall. Let's see if Mrs. Woods was home."

"You again," said Mrs. Woods to O'Connor when she opened the door. "It's the cops back again, Jim. Not got the policewoman with you this time?"

"She's busy on something else," said O'Connor. "Were you home last Monday afternoon, Mrs. Woods?"

"That afternoon? We sure were. Jim was still off work with the flu, and me waiting on him hand and foot. Why?"

"Did you happen to notice whether anybody went to the Leeds' apartment any time that afternoon?"

"I didn't see anybody, no." They were standing in the doorway facing her; past her plump person they could see the husband, comfortably tieless and shoeless, stretched out in a recliner chair, newspaper on his lap, watching and listening. "I won't say I would have, though. I was back and forth from the kitchen and then doing the laundry."

"You mean, any of those men used to come calling on Mrs. Leeds?" asked Woods interestedly. "I don't think there'd have been one on Monday, Officer."

"Why not?" asked Katz.

"Well, he was home. All afternoon. I was parked here right by the window, still feeling a little bit wobbly, so I wasn't moving around much. I saw him drive up and park about two-thirty—a little bit later, maybe—and he was home till about five-thirty. I saw him drive off."

"You sure of the time?" asked O'Connor sharply.

"That I am. I was just getting my appetite back, I said to Sarah, let's eat early, and we always eat about six, and it was about five-thirty she called me. And just then Leeds came out and drove away. He's got an old clunker of a Chevy, you can hear it a block."

"So, thanks very much," said O'Connor. On the doorstep of the apartment he blew off some steam. "Round and round and *round* the mulberry bush—when I think of the legwork I've done on this goddamned thing!" he said savagely. "Even before the autopsy report put us right back to the beginning—and all the goddamned while all we had to do was ask one simple question! Sweet Jesus! Simple! Like two plus two, for God's sake, and me chasing down all the lover boys—"

"But I wonder why," said Katz, "when he didn't give a tinker's dam about all the boyfriends?"

"I don't give a good goddamn why, but we'd better ask him," said O'Connor. They drove up to the liquor store on Glenoaks and collected Dudley Leeds without ceremony from behind the counter. The owner was there, and O'Connor stopped to fire just two questions: "Was Leeds here Monday afternoon, and why not?"

"Monday—he wasn't feeling good, thought he had a cold coming— he left at about two. But for God's sake, you don't mean—"

"Probably," said O'Connor. They put Leeds in the back of the Ford with Katz for company, and went back to the station. Leeds never said a word all the way.

Set down at the bare table in an interrogation room, Leeds just glowered at them and refused to say anything for a while. "I don't know how the hell you hoped to get away with it," said O'Connor. They had punctiliously read him all his rights. "It was right there plain to be seen once anybody with the brains of a two-year-old looked."

"You said it was probably one of the guys she went with," said Leeds.

"Well, we've changed our minds. Look, I'll spell it out for you, Leeds. The doctor told us she died well before six o'clock. You were home most of the afternoon. You left about five-thirty. You—"

"I told you where I was. I was—"

"At Damon's, and that alibi checked fine, only you don't need one for Monday night. It was Monday afternoon she got beaten up, and you were there. You were seen to leave at five-thirty. Now, that doesn't leave any damn much time at all for somebody else to have showed up and killed her, does it? Would you like to tell us why you did it?"

Leeds looked from one to the other of them, O'Connor standing over him with the jacket yanked back to show the shoulder holster, Katz with his keen, dark eyes cynical and interested. Suddenly Leeds exploded at them, "It was that goddamn Mex! If there's one thing I can't stand, it's a damn greasy Mex! We been arguing about it all week—I never meant to kill her, for God's sake! I was just so damn mad she wouldn't do anything!"

"About what?" asked Katz. "What Mex? One of the boyfriends?"

"No, goddamn it! Wilma had better sense than to pick up with a goddamn greaser! That Brenda! She never pays attention to me, but Wilma she'd listen to, I says to Wilma, for God's sake get her to get rid of that damn Mex! She says it's Brenda's own business. I says she's our kid, and by God I'd rather see her dead than with a Mex. Next thing, get married to the bastard—hell, I don't know what his damn name is—made me sick see her carry on with him, him coming to pick her up— I says to Wilma, you just tell her, and goddamn it, she keeps saying what's the odds, the Mex got some bread—I never meant to lay hands on her, but—"

"Back up," said O'Connor. "You came home because you had a cold. You got into the argument again."

"I came home *to* get into the argument. Going to get her to lay it on Brenda. We went at it all afternoon, and then she went to take a bath, she was going somewhere, and when she came out we went at it again, and she was mad then too and says I should damn well mind my own business, she ran into a pretty nice Mex the other day, and that was where I slammed it to her—I didn't mean to *kill* her, goddamn it, just give her a going-over! I didn't know she was dead till I came home and found the cops there. Goddamn it—"

They left him swearing, and they stood in the corridor. "It does make you tired," said O'Connor. "And we're supposed to be progressing? Human nature improving, for all the scientific wonders?"

"Human nature's like that French proverb: The more it changes, the more it stays the same," said Katz. "They'll call it involuntary manslaughter, and with luck he'll get a one-to-three."

And then for a breath they were silent, thinking about Fred Wayne.

"I'll call in about the warrant," said O'Connor shortly. "You take him over and book him. Then we can go and have lunch."

———————◆◆————————

Cindy Osborne called back at one o'clock to say that her brother and his wife were flying over; to ask about the body. Delia explained the procedure to her. "When—when should we know what it was?"

"We ought to have an autopsy report by Monday." It had probably been a heart attack. Delia had heard about Leeds from Katz and O'Connor, and felt a little annoyed at not being asked to sit in on the questioning. But they'd been working the case, it was perfectly natural. It was just that ever since she'd been here, she hadn't been doing anything so different from what she'd been doing for five years as a plain policewoman, except questioning witnesses. Oh, well, give it time and do her damndest to get them used to the female detective; maybe after a while she'd be solving cases too.

Poor and Forbes came in with one of their possibles for the heist and took him down the hall to talk to him. O'Connor and Katz came back at about two-thirty and asked if anything new had gone down. There was a report to type on Leeds; O'Connor rolled a triple carbon form into his typewriter and started that. He hated that typewriter, and Delia was convinced that it hated him for being so ham-handed. If he'd treat it with kindness and sympathy, give it a few soothing words and a little oil occasionally, it might not snap at him so often.

He was still sitting there swearing when keys jammed together and the spacer didn't work, when Varallo came in. He had Peter Santori with him, and left him in the doorway to stand over O'Connor.

"I'd be obliged if you'd try to scare him a little, Charles. None of the rest of us as well equipped for it."

O'Connor got up with alacrity. "What on?"

"Endicott," Varallo explained, and turning to get Santori, noticed Delia there. He hesitated, and then said, "OK, you can come and sit in too."

In an interrogation room, Varallo and O'Connor went on at Santori for some time, playing the classic game: gentle cop, tough cop. It didn't seem to have much effect on Santori, who had heard it before. He huddled there on the straight chair just looking miserable. He was a man of about forty-five, middle-sized, nondescript, with gray stubble on his cheeks and the unsteady hands of the drinker.

"Come on, Santori, get it over with and tell us about it—" O'Connor looming over him and giving the impression of being twice his size. The jacket was back, and the shoulder holster was in evidence.

"Down on Elm Street," and Varallo's tone was quiet and easy, their handsome blond Italian cop sounding friendly. "You thought it looked like a good bet—old house, cheap locks, garage empty. Have a quick look for any loot. Wasn't it that way? Last Sunday afternoon—"

Santori just shook his head. "Listen," said O'Connor roughly, "we haven't got all day! Let's hear about it!"

"Elm Street, that means something to you, doesn't it, Mr. Santori?" said Delia suddenly, quietly.

He looked up at her as if realizing she was there for the first time. When he spoke, his voice sounded husky, unused. "Yeah," he said. "Yeah, Elm Street means something to me. I used to own a house there—when I was married—before Millie died. A good job, and a car, and we had a good life. No kids, but a good life. But she died, and after that—nothing seemed to matter. I went to drinking, so I lost the job—and the house—and the car. And I went to stealing because I didn't want the charity—the welfare. Then. But after a while that kind of thing don't matter either." He turned and looked at O'Connor. "That's why Elm Street means something to me, cop. Not because I broke in some place there and hurt some old lady. You going to arrest me, or can I go back to my room? I got nearly a full bottle of port left."

They let him go.

———◄◆►———

Eileen felt, queerly, that she was marking time. Waiting. To see if the police came back? She didn't know.

Wesley went to his job, and she took the bus uptown and went to the library. She wanted to read the *Many Mansions* book again.

There was a copy in. She took it out, and did what she hadn't been able to do in two years. She stayed on the bus down to Los Feliz, got off, and walked over to the tall iron entrance gates of Forest Lawn. It was a clear, cold day, the sun bright. She walked over the lush grass to the great marble statue, where the swans floated on the pond, and sat there a long time, sometimes reading, sometimes just looking at the swans and the statue.

In late afternoon she walked back to the house. She'd like to get her watch fixed; it probably just needed cleaning. Mother Ruth had given it to her for her high school graduation. But Eileen never had much money, and Wesley always forgot to take it somewhere. Before, when she could get out, he had given her money every week, for the marketing. Since, he had given her a little money when she asked, and for the collection at church, or on the rare occasions when someone else had stayed with the old woman and she had gone uptown to shop for a new skirt, a pair of shoes. There was about five dollars in her purse now.

She got dinner, not paying much attention to what she chose. She wasn't hungry herself. He wasn't eating much, or talking to her at all. He went into the living room, where he had a small desk, and went back to work on his sermon.

About an hour later Mr. Dudey came.

Of all the people in the church, she had always liked the Dudeys best. They were nice people. Mr. Dudey was a salesclerk at Webbs' Mens' Store, tall and quite handsome, with a gray mustache and thin, gray hair. Mrs. Dudey, a little plump, was always cheerful-looking, with smiling eyes. Joy, who was a little older than Eileen, was a pretty, dark girl. If there had been time, she and Joy might have been friends, but Joy had a job, she was a stenographer at a loan company. It had always amused Eileen that Mr. Dudey had a little set ritual whenever he was introduced, or introduced himself. Fixing the new acquaintance with a compelling eye, he would say, "It is pronounced Doo-*dye*, you see. It is a Dutch name originally, I believe. Perhaps German, but I am more inclined to think Dutch. Doo-*dye*."

Joy had been the Sunday school teacher. Just last week she had told Wesley she couldn't take the class any more.

The doorbell startled Eileen. The police. But it was only Mr. Dudey, tall and neatly dressed and looking rather solemn. "Good evening," he said.

She was quite pleased to see him. "Come in. Do you want to see Wesley?"

"Yes, my dear." He sat down on the couch across from Wesley and began to talk to him. Wesley had finally taken the wheelchair out to the garage, and out of long habit she had dusted, straightened up in here, this morning; at least the shabby room looked reasonably neat. But Mr. Dudey wasn't looking for dust.

He talked well, concisely, clearly; he had it all set out in his mind, what he wanted to say.

"Mr. Endicott, I had better tell you at once that I have been named the spokesman for a certain majority of your congregation. We have had a great deal of serious discussion about several matters that have been troubling us, and I have been delegated to tell you plainly what decision we have reached."

"Oh," said Wesley. He wet his lips.

"First, I should like to make it plain to you that we offer our sincere condolences on the dreadful death of your mother. Whatever feelings have been aroused by that most unfortunate occurrence a couple of weeks ago, you do have our sympathy. But I should also make it clear that—although that may have in a sense brought matters to a head—in itself it was only the latest of a number of matters that have, um, been on our minds."

"I know—I know I couldn't take the place of the Reverend Hoby, he was here so long—but I've tried—"

"I daresay you have," said Mr. Dudey with some asperity. "But to put it plainly, Mr. Endicott, we don't feel that you have been satisfactory, or done the church much good. For instance, we have always held regular prayer meetings on Wednesday evenings, which you discontinued almost as soon as you took over the church—"

"I have to hold a job," said Wesley in weak self-defense. "I need the evenings to—to prepare my sermons. So few people ever came—"

"Mr. Endicott, surely any pastor worth his salt, so to speak, would not need every evening in the week to prepare a sermon! The church attendance has dropped drastically since you have been here. We used to have a full congregation every Sunday, fifty or sixty people. Now—"

"I know, I've felt it very much," said Wesley.

"We feel you could have done much more to persuade the backsliders. I'm very sorry to be the one to tell you all this, sir, but in plain language we feel that you're too young and inexperienced to bear the responsibility of a church. As you know, ours is a small sect, we don't have many churches—"

"Eleven in California," said Wesley automatically.

"—And every one of them must be an active, positive force for making new converts, winning souls to Christ. This church has deteriorated sadly, Mr. Endicott. It is the only word for it. You must be aware of this yourself. We feel that, to be blunt about it, you have not served an apprenticeship sufficient to prepare you to be a strong leader in the church."

"You never accepted me—liked me. I know you were used to the old minister—"

"Yes, sir, and we were grieved to lose the Reverend Hoby, but quite prepared to accept a new pastor, perhaps with fresh ideas, energy, positive programs to strengthen the congregation. You haven't done that, Mr. Endicott. But you're young—"

"I'm twenty-eight!"

Mr. Dudey cleared his throat. "I'm just to put it to you, sir, that we feel you haven't done your job and your duty as pastor of this Word of God Mission. I'm very sorry, we're all very sorry. But we have drafted a letter to the board of deacons to that effect. Perhaps in time, with more experience, guided by some older pastor—but that must be left in the hands of God. All I—"

"And the board of deacons!" Wesley flapped his hands at him in nearly hysterical gesture; his face went crimson. "They know what everybody should do—and not do— No money to fix the furnace, everybody complaining, it wasn't *my* fault—telling me I should compromise Christian principles to get that foolish woman to join the congregation because of her money—hypocrites, those people said to Mother, whited sepulchers—the *things* said to her, I don't say she was right, of course not, but intolerance and malice—all of you hypocrites as bad—"

"Mr. Endicott, I've said what I came to say." Mr. Dudey stood up. "I'm very sorry you have taken it like this. I can only say we have acted to the best of our beliefs and experience for the good of the church and our principles of Christian fellowship."

Wesley put his head down on the desk. Mr. Dudey waited a moment and said to Eileen, "I'm so sorry, my dear." He let himself out the front door.

And she was, now, sorry for Wesley—poor, ineffectual, struggling Wesley. He had tried. He was a silly little man, but he couldn't help being what he was.

She said, "I'm sorry, Wesley. They'll take the church away from you, won't they?"

He didn't raise his head. "You—you *bitch!*" he said chokingly. "You *murderess.* Leave me alone!"

Rhys and Hunter had just come into the office at eight o'clock when they got a call. A new body, said Patrolman Fenner.

"I can remember when you didn't get a homicide but about once in three months," said Rhys. They went out to look at it, and found Patrolman Fenner and an excited citizen waiting. It was down on Adams Street.

"Homicides all over these days," said Fenner. "But this one's probably a natural death. This is Mr. Keppel."

"Bill Keppel, I live up at the corner. Look, I was just out with these petitions, I'm a member of TRIM, Tax Reform Immediately, I was going door-to-door with these petitions, lower property taxes, and I just thought I'd try the old fellow, he signed a petition for me once before—"

You could hardly see there was a house there, it was so overgrown with shrubbery roof high. "What I gather, he was kind of a recluse," said Fenner. "Paul Jensen. In his seventies. Nobody knew much about him. Lived here for years."

"Lord, yes," said Keppel. "We bought the house in 1960, he was here then, had been for years. You didn't see him out much. Poor old guy, I guess no relatives. There was some talk that he had money, but I don't know about that. See, I came up to ring the bell. I had a flashlight, of course, and brother, did I need it in all that jungle—he never did anything in the yard, just let it all grow—and I saw there weren't any lights in the house. I thought maybe he goes to bed early, and then I saw the front door was wide open, and I thought, my God, an old fellow like that, maybe dropped dead—so I thought I'd better look—"

"And he had," said Fenner. "What it looks like. Some time back. It's one for you boys, all right."

They went in to look. It was probably the oldest house on the block, an old bungalow looking ready to fall down; maybe all the shrubbery was holding it up. Fenner had switched on the lights in the living room. It was a long combination room, living-dining, with an old-fashioned built-in buffet in the dining end.

"Oh, my God," said Hunter sickly.

Rhys had seen a few more corpses. "Dead some time all right," he said. The corpse was on the floor in the living-room area: a grossly decomposed corpse. If it had been summer, it would have been found sooner; as it was, the weather cold and windows closed, it had lain and decomposed. "A month?" said Rhys. "More? God knows. Let the doctor guess. This one, we needn't call the lab boys out on overtime. It'll keep till daylight. Seal the door and leave it for the day men."

CHAPTER 7

On Sunday morning, after approximately four hours' sleep, O'Connor got an excited Maisie into the car and drove up into the hills above Glendale College, and turned her loose. He could, of course, have done it every day. She galloped and circled and bounded like a dervish, her topknot flying and her banner of a tail high, coming back now and then to leap up and kiss him wetly. Once she caught him off balance and knocked him flat on his back.

At the top of the third hill, he sat down on a rock to catch his breath, lit a cigarette, and let her go. She wouldn't go down the hill, toward traffic, while he was here. He just hoped she wouldn't nose out any more unsavory bodies, the way she had last June.

He wondered if anything new had gone down overnight.

———◆———

One of the petty annoyances of the job, of course, was not only the deadly dull routine but also that new routine was always turning up to do. On Sunday morning, they had a look at the night-watch report and found the new one; Poor and Forbes had dredged up quite a list of possible suspects on the heist, and gotten back to that routine, while Varallo and Katz went to look at the place on Adams Street. Rhys said, probably a natural death; but they'd have to locate anyone to notify, do the paperwork on it.

They talked to Bill Keppel and a couple of other neighbors. Paul Jensen had evidently been a queer old fellow, something of a hermit, nobody knew much about him. The doctor would eventually tell them how he died; right now, they wanted to find out about any relatives.

Rhys had sealed the front door; they broke the seal and went in, and Katz said, "Yi," wrinkling his nose. The sweet stench of death would be there for some time. It was an old house, it was dirty and monumentally untidy. Some old men living alone would be fastidious; evidently Jensen hadn't been. There were clothes lying all over the two bedrooms; one bed wasn't made up at all, the other had a tangle of gray sheets, long unwashed, and blankets in a pile, as if its occupant never bothered to make it up. There were dirty dishes on the kitchen drainboard, empty beer cans all over the floor in the dining area and kitchen. Besides the original muddle, there was the inevitable result of the body being unfound so long: a mess of anonymous mouldy food on a couple of plates on the dining table. But there was enough evidence that Jensen hadn't exactly been a neat housekeeper.

"It's funny he wasn't found before," said Katz. "Even if there weren't any relatives or friends, you'd think the mailman would have noticed mail piling up. Everybody gets some." They looked in the mailbox; it was empty. There was an ancient Ford in the garage.

"Well, so maybe he had a box at the post office. We'll ask." Nowhere in the old, dirty house did they find an address book, an old letter, anything personal like that.

"Poor old guy," said Katz. "Looks as if he didn't have a soul to care about him. I wonder what he lived on." They hadn't spotted anything of much value, and no money. Of course, he may have had a wallet on him. The morgue wagon had already collected the body, for which they were grateful.

They'd have to wait to see what the doctor said, if any indication about relatives might be in a wallet on the body. If nothing showed up in the way of relatives, assets, the city would pay for a funeral, and the state appropriate the house if he'd owned it.

They went back to the office, and Katz said amiably he didn't mind doing the report.

———◆———

"We shall sing hymn No. 60: 'Take Up Thy Cross.'"

Harriet Meecham attacked the organ fumblingly, and a thin chorus of voices raised.

There were only ten people at the service this morning. Mrs. Meecham sat in a front pew, looking discontented. Miss Feller was there with her nearly senile mother, and the Haskells, and old Mr. Willard, who always came and slept through most of the service, and the Cliffords. Stella Clifford sat between her two sons; she kept looking around the church as if she couldn't believe it was so nearly empty. She was tightly corseted, wearing a pancake of a hat decorated with purple flowers. Dexter Clifford was fat and soft-looking, with a vacuous smile; Stanley was an ugly lump of a boy, uncomfortable in suit, shirt, unaccustomed tie, his acne-scarred face sullen.

They had joined raggedly in the mutter of ritual, "believe in the Father, the Son, the Holy Ghost." The last doleful verse of the hymn died, and the organ stopped with a wheeze.

Wesley stood up at the altar. His voice sounded thin in the emptiness of the little building. "Let the congregation confess all its sins. Almighty God, we have strayed like lost sheep. We have fallen into temptation. We have offended Thy laws." The few voices repeated obediently. "Have mercy upon us. Absolve Thy people, Lord." A pause, a few smothered coughs; he glanced out over the thinly populated pews. "Let us repeat the Lord's Prayer together."

They stood up with a small rustle, waiting his lead; when it failed to come, old Mr. Haskell embarked on a sonorous, "Our Father, Who art in heaven—" and they hastened to chime in.

Eileen was sitting as usual in the front pew on the right at the very end, where the wheelchair could stand in the aisle. Most of her mind was shut off from the service, which would go on for some time. This was the place where the minister was supposed to mention parish affairs and activities, but there hadn't been any to mention for a long time. There would be another hymn, and the texts read from Scripture, and the offertory, and Harriet Meecham would play more hymns while the collection was taken—only there wasn't anyone to start the little baskets around today, as Mr. Dudey and Mr. Beck always did—and then the sermon, and another hymn, and the closing prayer.

But quite suddenly he was saying in a sharper tone, "We shall sing hymn No. 104, please." There was a flutter of pages. Harriet Meecham said audibly, all flustered, "Oh dear, I don't know this one, I can't—" and plunged blindly at the keys. The organ stammered, and the voices rose uncertainly, ragged on an unfamiliar tune.

> Have Thine own way, Lord! Have Thine own way!
> Thou art the potter, I am the clay,
> Mold me and make me after Thy will,
> While I am waiting, yielded and still!
>
> Have Thine own way, Lord! Have Thine own way!
> Search me and try me, Master, today!
> Whiter than snow, Lord, wash me just now,
> As in Thy presence humbly I bow!
>
> Have Thine own way, Lord! Have Thine own way!
> Wounded and weary, help me, I pray!
> Power, all power, surely is Thine,
> Touch me and heal me, Savior divine!

As the organ faltered to silence, excruciatingly off-key, he leaned over the altar and tried to speak; his hands on the open Bible were shaking, and he made two attempts before he said abruptly in a breathy voice, "There will be no sermon today, my friends. Some of you may know that—that this church will soon have another pastor. I can—I can—" he faltered, and finished rapidly, "I can only wish him God's guidance in leading his people." And even more abruptly he turned and stepped down and blundered for the rear door of the church. It slammed behind him with a dull sound.

After a stunned moment, they began to talk to each other. Eileen got up unobtrusively and followed Wesley out the back, before they remembered she was there and began to question her.

She didn't want to be in either place, church or house, but at least Wesley wasn't talking to her.

He was standing quite still in the middle of the living room. He was trembling all over. As the screen door gave a faint squeak as she laid a hand on it, he suddenly cried, "Get out—get out!"

"Wesley—" But it was the cat. The cat had gotten in; it was warmer today and sunny, she had left the bedroom window open, and there was a rent in the screen. Wesley snatched up the box from the end table by the couch and flung it clumsily at the cat, and then dodged past into the back bedroom and slammed the door.

"It's all right," said Eileen to the cat, who had fluffed his tail. "Just a silly man." She felt a deep, remote sadness for Wesley, but there was nothing she could do for him, nothing he would let her do for him. She sat down on the couch, and the cat came to her. She stroked him and thought about Miss Morgan and Coco, and Wesley's incomprehensible God.

It was Mrs. Lacey who had brought Miss Morgan to the church, very proud; there was supposed to be a special grace in gaining converts, and Miss Morgan was reputedly rich. At least, she didn't work and had a big house in La Cañada, which she paid Mrs. Lacey to keep clean for her. And it had seemed she might join the church, perhaps give it some money. She was a large, blond woman with a nervous laugh and fussy clothes, but her eyes were very kind. She had talked about joining; and then her little brown poodle Coco had been run over, and she had come weeping to Wesley for consolation.

"They are looked after—over there—aren't they? I know his dear little soul is safe, I'll see him again—but I miss him so, Mr. Endicott—if I could be sure he's happy—"

And of course Wesley had told her that animals have no souls, she was foolish to hold such vain thoughts. She should have been a comic figure, standing there blinded by tears, hiccuping on little sobs, but there was a pitiful dignity to her— "It's a wicked lie—never believe in your kind of God if you think—it's cruel—"

How they had gone at him, thought Eileen. Driving away a new member. Could have compromised. Money.

She felt the warm thrum of purr under her hand. She whispered to the cat, "You do have a soul, don't you, darling? Maybe a nicer soul than mine. You couldn't look so wise if you didn't have a soul."

The cat's great green eyes met hers steadily, and his smile was bland.

———◆———

"You know," said Delia, "we never did talk to any of the people at the church, after I got the list. Do you think there's any reason?"

"Back to the possible personal quarrel. We're not making much progress with the burglars," said Varallo. "I think we've run it into the ground, just about. We looked at the idea of a personal motive, but it was never very likely. I suppose we could go talk to some of them, if you want to waste the rest of Sunday afternoon." He didn't sound enthusiastic.

"Well, I think I might. You can go and lean on Esteban Garcia again. Let me do some bloodhounding on my own."

Varallo shrugged. "Good experience, maybe. Not to throw cold water, but when you've been at this job as long as I have, you get feelings about it—a case smells this way or that way. And this one smells to me like the irrational, impersonal thing."

"Each to his own," said Delia blithely. She rummaged for the list in her handbag and went out.

Picking names at random, she looked up a Mrs. Muriel Shaw. Mrs. Shaw said she hadn't been back to that church in quite some while, she used to go because it was close by, she could walk, but she didn't care for the new young preacher. He was kind of a dim young man, not like the old one. Delia went on and found Mr. and Mrs. Kerr at home. They told her they'd belonged to the Word of God church for years, but it just wasn't the same with Mr. Endicott as with the old reverend. What had finished them finally was the day his mother was so rude to that man, and he didn't seem to take any firm stand at all; they'd been surprised that there were even a few narrow-minded people who stood up for her. Un-Christian it was. They'd found a Baptist church where the minister preached pretty good sermons. And no, they said, they hadn't gone to see the minister about it. Probably any of those who had were the ones who agreed with Mrs. Endicott. Just a terrible thing, someone murdering the woman, but maybe it had been the justice of God punishing her.

A waste of time, thought Delia, and Varallo was probably right. But looking over the list, she found Mr. Dudey, and entranced by the name, went to find him. It was a comfortable old bungalow on Harvard, and all the Dudeys were home.

"—Pronounced Doo-*dye*," he told her firmly. "It is a Dutch name originally. Possibly German, but I feel more probably Dutch. Doo-

dye." She liked the look of the whole family. They let him do the talking.

"The man's a fool," he said roundly. "We gave him plenty of time —young, inexperienced fellow straight out of divinity school, we thought perhaps he'd settle down, gain more confidence. And one doesn't go to church to be entertained, but one does like a solid, sensible sermon with some meat in it. Ah, well, it's a great pity, but as I told him, all our churches must have positive leadership." She heard about the letter to the board. "That business of his mother, so rude to that fellow, the smallest incident, but there's no denying it did create a schism in the congregation."

"We didn't care very much for the Endicotts from the first," said Mrs. Dudey. Her eyes were troubled.

Joy spoke up. "Not them, maybe, but I think Eileen's nice."

"Not much to say for herself," grunted Mr. Dudey.

"She's a little shy, I think, but nice. I'd like to have known her better," said Joy firmly.

A big fat waste of time, thought Delia. And it was nearly the end of her shift.

She checked in at the office. Poor and Forbes, at the dogged routine that so often paid off, had just dropped on the right heist man. It was funny, said Forbes; a pro who'd never have opened his mouth, and no evidence at the scene; but he'd lifted the clerk's wristwatch along with the cash from the till, and it was a graduation present and had his name engraved on the back: The heist man had been wearing it.

Goulding looked in as a general exodus began. "Thanks so much for the new corpse. What you boys do come up with. I'll get to him tomorrow. I've done the Osborne woman—it was a massive coronary. The family can have the body any time."

———◄◆►———

On Monday morning, with Poor off, there were court appearances to make: Ricketts and Maggott were both to be arraigned. O'Connor and Forbes went to cover that, and Katz went down to the main post office to ask about Paul Jensen.

"Oh yes," said the assistant postmaster, after he'd inspected the badge closely and consulted a Xeroxed list. "Yes, he does have a box here— Did you say he's dead? I think this was the name Benson was asking about recently—he could tell you more about it than I can. I'll get him in."

"Him," said Benson after he'd looked at the badge. "Sure, he's got a box here. Had a box. Dead, is he? Well, that explains it. The mail's been piling up in it. He never got much, there's just about enough to fill it now, but it hasn't been picked up in over a month. We had an address for him and a phone, but we haven't been able to get an answer, trying to call him."

"Naturally not," said Katz. "Can I take a look at the mail?"

"You can *look* at it," said Benson, "but you can't have it without a court order. Property of the U. S. Postal Service."

"I know, I know," said Katz. "We'll get one."

————◆————

The autopsy report on Edna Osborne came up, and Delia called Cindy. They all showed up together; Richard Osborne, his wife, Kathy; and Cindy. They said the coroner's office had called about the body, they'd been making arrangements. Richard Osborne asked about the car.

"It's at the police garage. I don't know how much damage was done. You'll have to sign a release for it, Mr. Osborne."

He nodded. "The funeral's on Wednesday. I may be able to get it fixed up enough by then to drive back." In the midst of sudden death you did have to think about such mundane matters.

Varallo had come back from a few more abortive interviews with the burglars, and was looking harried, when they got a call at two-forty. A householder had surprised a daylight burglar and held him for the police; Judovic and Morris were on the scene. "Don't tell me, a break of some kind?" said Varallo. "Let's go look at him, Delia. Though we both know how many there are roaming around." When they got there, he looked more interested, hearing the story.

"I just had a couple of teeth filled, I took the rest of the day off," said the householder, whose name was Goldstein, who was a stockbroker downtown. It was a big new house on Crestshire Drive. "I've got one of these automatic garage-door openers, I don't suppose he heard me drive in, over at the other side of the house. Damn it, it cost me four hundred bucks for the best locks you can buy, I didn't think anybody could break in here—came wandering back to the bedroom, and there this bastard was, cleaning out my wife's jewelry —and by God, he picks up a chair and tries to knock me out with it! That," said Goldstein, suddenly chuckling, "was where he made his mistake. He knocked me down, all right, but I fell on top of him." Goldstein must weigh around 250. "While he was trying to get his breath I tied him up with my belt and called you."

"He had some ID on him," said Judovic, handing over a wallet. There was a California driver's license for James Eustace, an address in San Francisco.

"So," said Morris, "I swung around a few blocks looking and found a car registered to him parked a block away on Tambor. It's a new Volvo."

"Helpful," said Varallo. Goldstein was looking at Delia interestedly. "We'll want a statement from you, Mr. Goldstein. Maybe you can come in to the station tomorrow."

"Sure, sure. Glad to. I just thank God I did walk in on him and he didn't get away with all the wife's diamonds. But after what I paid for locks on this place—"

It had been a very pro, slick job. He had gotten the sliding glass door on the patio pried open just far enough to reach in with a pair of tongs and pick out the metal bar holding it shut. Rather a new technique, and getting commoner.

They let Judovic bring Eustace in to the station, and took him down to an interrogation room. "Let's see what's in your pockets," said Varallo. Eustace hadn't volunteered anything. He was a thin, dark man of about forty with cold, dark eyes, and he was very sharply dressed in sports clothes. Silently he emptied his pockets onto the table; he'd been through this routine before. The only interesting thing was a receipt for a motel room, The Golden Key downtown.

Varallo didn't waste much time talking to him. It was evident that Eustace was an old hand; there'd be some record on him somewhere. Eustace just said flatly, "So OK, which way's your slammer? I hope you check me in before chow, I missed lunch." Varallo took him over to book him in.

"Be interesting to see what his package looks like when we trace it down." He wasn't in Glendale's records. "But considering the violence offered to Goldstein, I could just bear to know—if we can find out—whether he was around town a week ago Sunday. Not that it'd do us any good. That old a hand isn't going to tell us anything he doesn't have to, and even if he was here, not one damn thing says he was down on Elm Street."

They went down to The Golden Key, showed the badges to the manager, and got co-operation. Eustace had been checked in since Saturday. He had a single room on the second floor. They went to look at it, and there was one neatly packed suitcase full of clothes open on the bed; another one, locked, was in the closet. "He said he'd be checking out tonight," said the manager.

Varallo put the locked suitcase on the floor, squatted beside it, and pried it open with his knife. There was newspaper spread out on top; he lifted it out, a whole day's Los Angeles *Times*.

"Good heavens!" said Delia.

"*E come,*" said Varallo. "Isn't that pretty." The suitcase was nearly filled with jewelry, just loose. Good jewelry. Gold shone in the afternoon sun; diamonds sparkled.

"My good God in heaven," said the manager.

"We'll give you a receipt for it," said Varallo. "But you know," he added to Delia in the car, "I doubt very much that Mr. Eustace the violence-prone daylight burglar was anywhere near Elm Street, or any street like it, in his life. Not at all his speed. The fancy big houses where he's likely to find the diamonds."

"And none of that loot's been reported to us."

"So we'd better ask around other forces who might have reported it."

———◆———

O'Connor had been busy getting that court order for Jensen's mail. It came through about four o'clock, and he took it down to the post office and brought back a small stack of mail to look at, tossing half of it over to Katz. "He didn't get much. I wonder how he managed to stay off the mail-order lists. Most days there's more junk mail than anything else."

"There's a place you can send to stop it," said Katz. "Look at this. Nice checks. Stock dividends. Modest, but adding up. Fifty, a hundred, ninety—"

"I've got a couple of hundred. And—" O'Connor had found a personal letter, the only one in the stack. It bore a return address, Bill Jensen, an address in Victorville. He slit it open. A single page of large, careless handwriting. "Dear Paul, How are you? Haven't heard in so long thot Id check in and ask if everythings OK with you. We are fine, business doing good. Sylvia says wed be glad if you could come visit but we know what a homebody you are. Write when you can, your brother Bill."

"Well, a relative at least," said O'Connor. He got through to Victorville and talked to Mrs. Jensen. She said Bill was at the station; well, his Shell service station, of course, and what was it about? O'Connor convinced her to give him the number, got hold of Jensen, and broke the news.

"Oh, my God," said Jensen. "My God. What was it, a heart attack or what?"

"We don't know yet, Mr. Jensen. He was just found on Saturday night, and it's only today we've been able to look at his mail and found your letter. I'm sorry to tell you he'd been dead some time, a month or more."

"Oh, my God," said Jensen. "What a thing. But I've got to tell you, Lieutenant, I'm not surprised. I was always afraid something like that would happen. Paul, he was an awful loner. He never married, didn't like any kind of socializing, far back as I remember he never had many friends, no close ones. And since he was retired— what?—oh, he used to have a little watch-repair place there in Glendale—I guess he didn't go out anywhere even as much as he used to. I hadn't seen him in ten years, since we moved up here. We'd have a little note maybe two or three times a year, and a Christmas card, that was all. And since he'd gotten older, we'd worried about him alone there, nobody to look in on him. He was seventy-four, ten years older than me."

"Well, that's about how we figured the setup."

"Look, I better come down there. Have to arrange a funeral and all. I don't know how he was fixed, he was always pretty close-mouthed about his affairs, but I can take care of it."

"He seems to have had some nice stock dividends coming in."

"Is that so? Well, thanks, Lieutenant. I can't pretend we were all that close, difference in age and all, but he was my brother, after all, and I'm right sorry to hear about this. I'll be down in a day or two to fix up about a funeral."

"And that is that," said O'Connor, putting down the phone. "Where have you two been?" as Varallo and Delia came in.

"Do come see what we picked up at the end of the rainbow," said Varallo. "Maybe we're starting to get a classier bunch of pros operating here, Charles. This one seems to be a real big-time jewel thief. I hope nobody tries to burgle the station while this is still on the premises."

"Oy-yoy, how pretty," said Katz when the suitcase was opened. "But no loot we've got on the books."

"No, we'll ask around."

O'Connor got home a little late, and surprisingly found the baby yelling blue murder. Usually at this hour he was quiet. "I think he must be teething," said Katharine, sounding harassed. "He's been at it most of the afternoon. And Maisie thinks it's my fault. I put him down a while ago to get his bottle, and she stood guard over him and showed her teeth at me when I came back."

"Don't tell me he's going to start yelling all evening now? My God," said O'Connor, "this is getting to be more of a project than I bargained for. If I'd had any idea what babies were like—"

"Now, Charles. They do grow up eventually into people."

She finally got him settled and they had a peaceful, if late, dinner. But it was, as O'Connor said, the suspense that worried him. That kid had a built-in time clock. And the clock in the bedroom had a luminous dial. They went to bed, and he couldn't get to sleep. Close his eyes as resolutely as he would, he kept finding himself staring at the dial, and eventually the hands reached 2 A.M. and he lay waiting for it.

Silence. He thought he could hear Maisie snoring from the living room.

More silence. Katharine stirred at his side. "Any second," muttered O'Connor.

Nothing. "He isn't going to," whispered Katharine.

"Oh, you beautiful dreamer," said O'Connor.

"But he's not." Continued silence.

He didn't. It was a miracle. But neither of them could get to sleep, and consequently when they did, they slept through the alarm, and O'Connor never got to the office until after nine o'clock.

When he did, he walked into a madhouse.

———————◆———————

That was another thing about the job. It was erratic; you could never predict what was coming next.

The night watch had been busy. They had left the day men two new heists, at a drugstore and a liquor store. There had been a new burglary reported after the night watch had gone off. The heist at the liquor store had happened just before closing time, and the owner said the heist man had put one hand on the counter to jump over it with the gun, so Rhys had sealed the door. Burt had been chased out first thing to see if there were any liftable latents on the counter. They were short one man; Forbes was off.

Poor had gone out on the burglary. Katz had gone to bring the drugstore clerk in to make a statement and look at mug shots. Varallo was talking to the liquor store owner when O'Connor came in and heard all the news.

"Why the hell can't things happen one at a time?" he demanded querulously. "Maybe Joe's right, the moon sets people off."

"There isn't a full moon for two and a half weeks—no, more," said Delia, looking up from her typewriter. "New moon next Monday, I think. Joe was marking the almanac."

Katz came in with a long, lank citizen in tow and sat him down beside his desk and started to talk to him. At this point Dr. Goulding appeared in the doorway.

"Hah!" he said, surveying all the activity in the big detective office. "Busy?" His cadaverous long face, topped by the gleaming bald head, wore a brief expression of fiendish glee. "I'm going to make you busier. Jensen was stabbed to death."

"Oh, sweet Jesus Christ!" bellowed O'Connor, outraged. "Now, that is all we needed, another homicide to do all the legwork on! Holy saints and angels—"

"Don't yell at me, I didn't do it." Goulding sat down beside his desk and lit a cigar. Katz and Varallo came up to hear the story. "It's impossible to say just when, he's been dead at least a month and possibly six weeks. As far as I can make out, he was a healthy old codger, no sign of any heart condition, diabetes, lung congestion— little arthritis, which was only natural. Might have lived to be a hundred. And the autopsy was one hell of a job, but I can tell you this and that. He'd been struck several blows to the face, and also stabbed in the back and chest. With two different knives."

O'Connor groaned. "You've got to make it so complicated!"

"Sorry, but there it is. There were three back wounds. A knife about seven inches long with a blade about an inch and a half wide. Four chest wounds. A knife about ten inches long with a blade about three-quarters of an inch wide. One of the chest wounds did it —straight into the heart, but it was probably just chance, no indication of any anatomical knowledge. He'd eventually have bled to death internally from the other wounds, but as it was, that one put him out, bang, right now. You'll get an official report, but I just thought I'd come and tell you. Business picked up again, has it? Well, it never rains but it pours," said Goulding cheerfully.

"Of all the goddamned times to have one like this come along—" O'Connor yanked at his tie and pulled it loose.

Burt poked his head in the door. "Thought you'd like to know I lifted a dandy set of latents off the counter at the liquor store. Partial palmprint too. I'm just about to see if we know 'em."

"Here, Rover," said O'Connor. "You've got another job. The hell of a job. You and Thomsen—"

"Listen, we've got to check these out."

"All right, all right, but then you and Gene go and have a good, long, hard look at the Jensen place—"

"The chief's place?" Burt was surprised. "On what?"

"No, no, a new homicide, goddamn it, for our sins. Of all the—"

Poor came in with a couple of indignant citizens. The woman was saying in a high, angry voice, "And my new mink coat and the tape recorder John gave me for Christmas and all the sterling, a complete set for twelve, and it belonged to my mother—"

"Just take it easy, Mrs. Goodman. We'll get a list made up."

"Oh, my God!" said O'Connor. "There's this damn burglary too, and they'll have to check for prints—"

"Preserve calm, Charles. Most of us can double in brass, know how to dust for prints. It'll all get done eventually."

The liquor store owner was vague on description; it had all happened so fast, he said. The drugstore clerk spent all morning looking at mug shots and didn't make any. Thomsen went out to print the Goodman house. The Goodmans had been in Palm Springs visiting friends the past week, had gotten home after midnight and discovered the burglary, which could have happened any time in the past seven days, and they were still annoyed that the detectives hadn't come roaring right out to investigate it. None of the loot matched anything in the suitcase from the motel.

Burt developed the liquor store prints, had a look in their records without any luck, and sent them to LAPD and the FBI. He went out to the Jensen place about noon to join Thomsen in going over the whole house. Thomsen hadn't picked up any strange prints at the Goodmans', and both the Goodmans had raised hell about having their prints taken by the police.

At ten minutes to four, LAPD called to say that the heister's prints were in their files. He was Luis Echeverria, quite a little pedigree, they'd send his package over if Glendale wanted it. They supplied a last known address immediately: Collins Street in North Hollywood.

Last known addresses were not always productive, but it was a place to start. Poor and Varallo were the only ones in except Delia when that came through, so they took Poor's Rambler in case Echeverria was there, and started for North Hollywood. "I think that's why you got that compact," said Poor. "Use everybody else's car to transport suspects."

Unfortunately, as it turned out, Luis Echeverria was there. He was in the midst of a large and apparently loving family, and when two cops showed up to arrest him on a felony charge, they all joined in to save Luis from persecution. Mama and Grandma took on Poor with a broom and an iron frying pan, while Papa and a younger brother tackled Varallo, with Luis fleeing out the back door. Varallo cut down Papa after a wild swinging match, dodged the young brother, and took out after Luis, only to be ambushed by an unsuspected little sister, who stuck a shovel between his legs and sent him sprawling over a horseshoe pitch in the backyard. Poor, escaping the females with blood running down his face from a cut on the head, caught up to Luis as he was climbing into a vintage T-bird and brought him down with a flying tackle.

"Compacts," said Varallo breathlessly, feeling his nose, "hell, John. We'll need a bus to take them all in." They called up a couple of black-and-whites to ferry them in to jail: The rest of them would be charged with interfering with officers in pursuit of duty, and let loose the day after a court appearance. Both Varallo and Poor spent a little while in First Aid.

When he came in the back door, Laura let out a little shriek. "Don't panic," said Varallo. "Only a couple of black eyes. I thought my nose was broken, but it isn't. Just swollen."

"Oh, you just had to be a cop again, didn't you?" said Laura resignedly. "Really, Vic, you are a sight. What happened?"

"And I'll be a worse sight tomorrow. But just wait, *amante*, till you hear about Charles' miracle. Have we got any aspirin? At least it's my day off tomorrow."

———◆———

Over Tuesday night there was another heist. Wednesday was fairly hectic, with Varallo and Delia off, the continued hunt for the possible suspects out of Records. It was two o'clock when Katz came back to the office after questioning another one, who turned out to have an alibi, and noticed the suitcase still sitting beside Varallo's desk.

"Yi!" he said to himself. The loot—in the press of business they'd never gotten to that. He got on the phone and started calling. NCIC had turned up a record on Eustace with both the Chicago police and

San Francisco. But with Eustace at the motel here, this loot had probably come from some place around, and recently. He hit paydirt on his second call, to Pasadena. A Detective Elliott said, "Hey. Hey, sure—we had a big haul reported, last Saturday night. Movie producer's pad up toward the hills. I've got a list—"

It checked with the loot in the suitcase. Katz's father was a jeweler; he knew something about stones, design, and could match up the pieces with Elliott's description over the phone. "Well, we've got him," he told Elliott. "Priority. They can't have the sparklers back for a while—evidence."

"I know, I know. They'll be annoyed," said Elliott. "Can't be helped. Thanks for cleaning one up for us."

———◆———

On Thursday morning, with Katz off, the other heist still being worked, the burglary with no handle but the possible random suspects from Records, O'Connor was feeling harried. There had been a brawl in a bar last night with a man knifed, the knifer in custody, but it made more paperwork. Poor had gone out hunting possibles on the remaining heist. O'Connor was just saying to Varallo, "We'd better stick that burglary in Pending now, there's no point in wasting time on it," when Burt came in.

"We've picked up the hell of a lot of odds and ends at the Jensen place, Charles. I got the doctor to chop his fingers off and we've got 'em soaking, hope to get some reliable prints for comparison. But there were other people in that house—at least two, maybe more. I've got twenty-six good prints, and I think some of 'em are a woman's. All sorts of different places—refrigerator, bedroom chest, coffee table, closets. It looks as if the place was ransacked. And there's a woman's hat with blond hairs in it. Two blood-stained knives on the kitchen counter; they could match up with ones the doctor described. No prints on these, but they're rough handles. But the blood type's AB which matches Jensen's."

"All right!" said O'Connor. "Look, Vic—all this on hand to work. You've run the Endicott thing into the ground, there's no place to go. Shove it and forget it."

"I knew that three days ago," said Varallo. The black eyes had developed beautifully; he looked like an Italian sunset, but it'd be fading by tomorrow. "The anonymous thing, never much chance we'd drop on that X. Shove it."

The desk buzzed O'Connor. Duff said, "You've got a new homicide. By what Morris says, a teen-age OD."

"Oh, for God's sake," said O'Connor. "More paperwork!"

———— ◄◆► ————

Sergeant Duff plugged wires into the switchboard, monitoring traffic calls. Pretty soon Glendale was going to have to have more than a desk sergeant taking traffic calls, relaying calls to the front office. He had an emergency call from a traffic unit, reporting a paramedic call. These punk kids, he thought. O'Connor came downstairs with Varallo and went out.

Forbes came downstairs and stopped to light a cigarette. "Keeping us busy," he said.

"Say it again," said Duff. "That last call—probably something for you. Felony hit-run, I guess. Those damn motorcyclists—maybe they've killed somebody now. The parking lot attendant, that lot on lower Maryland—"

"All we needed, something else," said Forbes, and went out.

CHAPTER 8

Mr. Guiterman came at a little before ten o'clock, agitated, apologetic, helpful, to tell her about the accident. He drove her to the hospital. "Those damn kids," he said. "It's mostly early mornings they been around, before the bank and stores open, making a speedway of the alleys down there, the parking lots. I'd just gotten there, was talking to your husband, when they showed up and I called the cops —listen, I feel terrible about this, Mrs. Endicott—"

"It wasn't your fault."

"No, but damn it, I'd just fired him. I couldn't help that either— but, my God, those kids—roaring around from Broadway, and the squad car came in the other direction and kind of boxed them in the lot, a couple of them, and this one swerved right up where we were standing and—my God! But they got him, he crashed his bike on the back end of the building, I guess he was hurt too. But look, your husband's being taken care of fine, those paramedics were right on the job. Look, I couldn't help it, about the job, Mrs. Endicott."

"People complained, about his handing out the tracts?"

"Oh that—no, it wasn't that. I only manage that lot and a few others, and there's been some new regulations put in. It just never crossed my mind to ask him, when he got hired, but now they want drivers' license numbers, and it turns out he doesn't drive—all lot attendants got to be licensed drivers. I'm sorry, but you see how it is. And I want you to know, set your mind at ease, there's insurance— I'd given him two weeks' notice, he was still working, still covered— the medical expenses, that'll be OK." He was bald and stout and kind, really sorry.

He was a help at the hospital; the red tape, all the forms to be filled out. He said, after that while they waited in a little alcove down the hall, "Listen, Mrs. Endicott. I know these emergencies can be rough. His two weeks' pay was due, I got the check in my pocket, but no telling if he could endorse it right away. You'd rather, I can give you the cash." Two hundred and eighty dollars.

He waited with her for some time until a doctor appeared and told them about Wesley. The doctor was impersonal, efficient, wasting no time. "There's a compound fracture of one leg, some ribs broken, a concussion. I don't believe there are internal injuries, but we're still waiting for the X rays. He's still unconscious, and in any case we'd have to sedate him to set the leg— I wouldn't expect him to be fully conscious until tomorrow morning, and there's no reason for you to wait around here."

"But he'll be OK?" asked Mr. Guiterman.

"Oh yes. Take a little time to mend." The doctor strode off. Mr. Guiterman said he'd take Eileen home.

On the way, she thought about the money in her bag; the wad of cash, more than she'd ever seen at once. But money now— there wasn't much food in the house. And she didn't know when there might be any more money. She asked him to let her off at the Safeway, said no, she'd get home all right, it was only three blocks. He had really been very kind. She shopped carefully for the least expensive things: spaghetti, thick soups, potatoes, milk, crackers, a loaf of bread, margarine.

When she got back to the little house and put everything away, she sat down on the couch in the living room and thought, what am I going to do?

Payment for what wrong one did.

Well, she thought with dreary practicality, I had a job once before, I can get one again. Some kind of job, waiting on people, doing something, if just housework. But now, when the church would be taken away from Wesley, there wouldn't be this little house. She had better get a paper, tomorrow, and look for a room, a small apartment —and, of course, the job. When Wesley got out of the hospital—

And, she thought starkly, did she owe anything at all to Wesley?

———————◀◆▶———————

Mail was still getting delivered to Jensen's post office box, and on Wednesday there had been a bill for a broker's commission, a Frank

Dart at Hornblower and Weekes. Varallo went to see him that
Thursday morning. Dart was distressed to hear about Jensen.

"Damn shame. Crime rate way up, all these wild ones running
around, and I know as soon as you pick 'em up the damn courts let
'em out. Well, he was a funny old bird. Pretty shrewd about the
market—he'd ask advice, didn't always take it, and he was usually
right. No, he never said anything to me about any relatives."

"We didn't come across any stock certificates. Do you know if he
had a safety-deposit box anywhere?"

"Oh sure. Security Pacific at Broadway and Brand, he banked
there. I'll wish you luck on catching up to whoever did it. Just the
hell of a thing."

Varallo verified the safety-deposit box, and set up the machinery
on that; an IRS man would meet somebody at ten Monday morning
to open the box. There hadn't been a wallet on the body, but they'd
found a ring of keys in the bedroom; the lockbox key was probably
on that.

He went back to the station, and on the stairs passed Poor and
Forbes shepherding a big lout of a kid wearing a bandage on his head
and on one arm, into the lobby. Upstairs, Varallo asked O'Connor,
"Who've John and Jeff caught up with?"

"It erupted just as we left. Felony hit-run. Those joy-riding motorcyclists. He got banged up too, they just brought him up from
Emergency a while ago." O'Connor was gloomily contemplating his
cigarette. "I picked up that Lilly"—one of the possibles on the heist
from Records—"and he's got an alibi. He was in a hot poker game
down in Gardena. Gave me the names of six pals who can back him
up."

"And you will never guess," said Delia, "who the joy riders clob-
bered. Little Mr. Endicott, at that parking lot. The traffic men said a
broken leg, whatever. He is having a run of bad luck, isn't he? The
church elders are going to take his church away from him, did I tell
you? Because he can't preach solid sermons and discontinued the
Wednesday night prayer meetings."

"The piece of chewed string," said O'Connor. "There's no kickback on those prints yet."

"I tell you, Charles," said Varallo, "I'm not holding my breath.
Nobody picked the Jensen house on looks as worthy of looting. I

think it's got to go right back to that neighborhood, where he'd lived so long, where the rumor had passed around that he had money, kept it in the house—the inevitable rumor about anybody old, living alone. He was a loner, didn't go out socializing—he wouldn't have been known outside the neighborhood. And nobody picked that place at random."

"I'd got there," said O'Connor. "Yeah. Wait for it—we still haven't heard from the feds—but it could have been a first time out for somebody."

"Several somebodies," said Varallo. "The two knives—and that hat—and that is what you might call a mixed neighborhood, Charles. Single houses, apartments, and a lot of small businesses not too far away up on Colorado. And any place he might have been known a little farther away, but what would that be?—the market where he got groceries. There's a Food Giant two blocks down Colorado."

"We can ask," said O'Connor. "I'm not usually a pessimist, but I've got the feeling we may never know the answer on this one."

Poor came back, sat down at his desk, and lit a cigarette. "That punk is feeling sorry for himself. Kept telling us if the damn squad car hadn't come at him he'd never have swerved and hit that guy. I just hope it teaches him a lesson. They'll probably suspend his license six months and nick him with a fine, too much to hope he'll serve any time on it. The whole bunch are Glendale college kids, old enough to know better."

O'Connor got up and straightened his tie. "Well, I suppose there are things we could be doing."

———◆———

When the nurse at that end of the wing came on duty at 7 A.M., she found the accident case from yesterday conscious. He was apathetic, accepted attention without asking for anything. But the second time she looked in there, answering another patient's bell, he called her weakly.

"Please," he said, "dying. Must—I must talk to—the police. Please call—his name is Varallo— Important I talk to him—"

The nurse didn't enlighten him about his condition; nervous patients often thought they were dying. She did know he was a traffic-accident case; it was possible he had some information for the police. On her next break she called the police station.

———◆———

"Now, why the hell does he want to talk to me?" said Varallo, annoyed when Duff relayed the call. "Hold his hand and reassure him the villain who did it is under lock and key?"

"He isn't," said Delia. "He made bail last night."

"Damnation," said Varallo. He drove over to the hospital, and they let him into the four-bed ward. The curtains were drawn all about Wesley Endicott's bed. Endicott looked up at tall Varallo standing close there; Endicott wore a remote expression. Only a pale stubble showed on his unshaven chin, and his voice was a thin whisper. He had one leg in traction, a bandage on his head.

"I made her—pull the curtain. Because I've got to tell you. Dying —want to clear my conscience—maybe make up to God for all my failures. I killed her. I did it—to Mother."

Varallo stared at him, wondering if he was delirious. "No," said Wesley, "you've got to believe me. I did. She—she was old and unhappy and—I did it. Listen to me, please—I want you to go tell Eileen—what I've told you. Will you—do that? That's all—I wanted to say to you." He shut his eyes and turned his head.

Now, what the hell is this all about? Varallo wondered. The little fellow going nuts. Varallo went out and found the nurse.

"Dying? He's a nervous little twit," she said scornfully. "He'll be all right if he doesn't worry himself into a heart attack."

And he wanted Eileen told. Well, damn it, Varallo was just startled enough, and curious enough about this to hear what Eileen's reaction might be. He drove over to the ugly little church and walked around to the house behind.

When she came to the door she had a newspaper in one hand, open to the classified ads. "Oh. You've come back," she said.

"Mrs. Endicott," he said frankly, "I'm damned if I understand this, but your husband has just confessed that he stabbed his mother. I don't think it's possible that he did, and I don't know why he's saying so. He asked me particularly to tell you about it."

She must have waited twenty seconds before she asked, "What—did he tell you?"

Varallo repeated it. "I don't believe it. Have you any idea why he said it, unless he's had a brainstorm?"

"Oh, yes," she said. She turned and went into the house and put the newspaper down on a chair. "That is just exactly the stupid sort of thing he would do, you see. Thinking he's being noble. Making a sacrifice. Thinking he'll improve his soul, or something, by saving me. Yes, he said it because he knows I killed her. I thought I could get out of paying for it—or pay for it some other time, maybe— but I see that wasn't meant either. I'm the one who did it."

"Would you like to tell me about it?" asked Varallo quietly.

"No. Not you. I'll tell that policewoman all about it," said Eileen. "You see, only another woman would really understand—why it happened. I'll tell her if you bring her here. Or if you want to arrest me first."

"Not all that rush," said Varallo. The phone was on the desk two feet away; he couldn't explain to Delia, just told her to come. He left Eileen lying back on the couch with her eyes shut, and was waiting outside for Delia when she showed up fifteen minutes later.

"What's going on? I thought we'd shelved Endicott."

"I don't know what the hell's going on." Varallo told her about it. "All I'll say is, this could be the answer. Let's hear what she's got to tell you."

———◆———

Eileen sat on the shabby couch, looking white and exhausted, and fixed her eyes on Delia and talked. Delia took shorthand notes; Eileen seemed not to notice. "—Thought I was going insane, you see. But then—when they told me what had happened, I knew. I knew how it must have been—I must have done it—just before. There was a kind of explosion in my mind—you see, I must have done it, because of the Dream. It was always there waiting for me—I knew someday I'd walk into it, when it was really happening. And that was the time. It was the Dream, when I walked in here that night. The policeman in his uniform with bright brass buttons"—her voice was almost dreamy— "and the cat on the chair, and everything they said. I could never hear everything they said in the Dream, just those things. *It was deliberate murder. There's nothing you can do for her now. We'll have to leave that to the detectives. I don't know why it had to happen.* And the absolute knowledge that it was all my fault—it had happened because of me.

"And I thought, maybe I'd paid for it already—but I see now it wasn't enough. It would have been so much easier if I'd just died with all the rest of them—"

Delia let that go. "Let's get this straight. You don't actually remember stabbing your mother-in-law? You had a blackout."

"It was just too much, all of a sudden. It was like—like a big black cloud all around me, but red too, and I was standing there with the scissors in my hand—that's the last I remember— And then I was on the walk outside, and it was later, the sun nearly down—"

"You don't remember anything in between?"

"No, it's all black. But you can see I must have done it. Nobody else hated her enough. Wesley never knew that—he was outside it— he never understood how hard it was. But he knew afterward I'd killed her. I suppose you want to arrest me now."

Delia looked at Varallo. He jerked his head at her; they went outside to the meager brown-grassed space behind the church. "Well?" said Delia.

"*Per l'amore di Dio!*" said Varallo. He was looking annoyed. "Now, that is really the limit! No, we're not about to arrest her. No way. This is a very tricky little play here, and it could be intended just that way, and I damn well don't like it. I said this felt to me like the irrational thing, the moment's loss of control. I still do, and I think she did do it, just about the way she says. The old lady yelled for her just once too often, and she saw red, and she had the scissors in her hand, and *addio*. On the convenient amnesia I have reservations."

"What about him? Why did he do such a harebrained thing?"

"Probably just why she said. Being noble, death-bed confession.

Far, far better thing I do. He's impractical—unworldly. But that's the first thing about it, you know. Here we've got two confessions. Legal confusion. Nobody's going to like it except a defense lawyer."

"He can't have done it. Actually, or emotionally. He wouldn't have the guts, and besides we can probably show that he was on a bus or somewhere."

"Can we? In any case, two confessions. And can you imagine what the defense lawyer would do with the amnesia?"

"I certainly can," said Delia. "But that's the part of it I believe. It was all too much, right then, and she went into a kind of traumatic shock. Blackout. Symbolical, I have to get away from this."

"Or," said Varallo cynically, "when she heard that saintly Wesley had confessed all to save her soul—mistaking himself for Jesus Christ, maybe—it occurred to her that he couldn't inherit under the will if that goes on record, and she's taking the chance of a short term."

"Don't let the tough-cop cynicism rule your reason," said Delia coldly. "That girl is painfully honest, and she doesn't have that kind of mind. I wonder what she meant, she should have died with the rest. What do we do about this, then?"

"We go back and upset Charles with it. We don't make a move until we've talked to the DA's office. The courts are busy, and the DA isn't going to waste time and the taxpayers' money bringing a charge that'll never stick. Yes, I think she did it all right—it fits just dandy—"

"She can't remember doing it," said Delia.

"If you buy the amnesia bit. So all right, go all the way and believe the blackout. Isn't that natural too, that she wouldn't remember? Stick the scissors into the old lady, bang, traumatic shock, run away. And a beautiful case of diminished responsibility it is. This way or that way."

"I'd like to talk to her some more," said Delia.

Varallo eyed her. "I suspect you're feeling sympathetic. Don't, lady. Don't let your emotions loose on a case. If Wesley were a different character, I might smell collusion here."

"Don't be stupid," said Delia.

"You think so? There was a motive. The tiresome old lady and her money. No, I don't think it was like that. But before we decide what to do here, in such a legal tangle, we talk to the DA."

"What about the girl? She looks about at the end of her rope."

"Afraid she might suicide if we don't take her straight to jail?"

"No," said Delia thoughtfully. "No, I don't think so. I want to hear some more out of her."

"Rather you than me," said Varallo. "I'm going back to break this to Charles. What a mess." He turned away, and then turned back. "Another thing I don't like about it—recurring dreams! *Basta così!* That puts the lid on it!"

Delia watched his tall figure up the walk to the side of the church. As he got there, he nearly collided with a woman coming around the church. He stepped aside, and turned to watch her as she came toward the house. She stopped and looked at Delia. She was a woman in her middle fifties, very smartly dressed in a gray suit and scarlet blouse; she had neat pepper-and-salt hair, dark eyes, a long nose. "Who might you be?" she asked in a pleasant voice.

"Police," said Delia.

"Oh. About the accident, I suppose. You've come to see Eileen? Well, don't mind me, I'll wait until you're finished." They walked back to the house together and went in.

"Oh!" said Eileen. "Oh—I never—I never thought I'd see you again!"

"I didn't think I'd better come here. When you stopped coming to see me, I thought maybe you'd decided not to make any more friction at home."

"I couldn't come. You know I wanted to—it didn't matter what they thought—but she got worse, I had to be here all the time, there wasn't anybody else, none of the people at church offered to come much, and she didn't like that anyway, and we couldn't afford— I asked about practical nurses once, but it was too expensive—"

"You look as if you've been pulled through a knothole. You're twenty pounds underweight. Yes, I see. You've been stuck here with that obnoxious old woman day in day out for two years? My dear child—"

"And then I murdered her," said Eileen. And suddenly she began to cry convulsively, painfully, the sobs shaking her thin body.

She rocked back and forth in a paroxysm of sobbing. The other woman turned to Delia, sudden shock in her eyes. Delia just shook her head.

"Eileen—come on now, my dear—I want to hear all about it, and then we'll see what can be done." She sat down beside her and put an arm around her shoulders. Eileen gave a last great hiccuping sob and slid off the couch in a dead faint.

They got her into the bedroom and covered with a blanket; she looked ready to die. "She's skin and bones," said the other woman crossly. "That pair between them drinking her blood. Probably not enough to eat. How she ever got involved with that man—I'm Marcella Moore, by the way."

"Delia Riordan. Detective Riordan."

"Oh, really? I'm in business down on Broadway. I got to know her through that—that husband of hers, at the parking lot, you know." She had Eileen's feet propped up scientifically. "They wouldn't let me in the house, of course, but she used to come to see me—"

"Why not?"

"Oh, I encouraged her to read wicked books about reincarnation and astral travel and ghosts. That's right, dear, take your time. You're all right. Hadn't seen her in two years. I've been on vacation the past couple of weeks, just went into the shop this morning and heard about the accident—and his mother—from the other attendant." She didn't ask any questions about the homicide. "Lie still a bit, dear, you'll feel better in a minute. I'll bet you haven't had a bite today. I'm going to get some hot soup down you, if there's such a thing in the house."

"Some—in the left-hand cupboard," said Eileen. "But don't— don't go away. I want to tell you— Never anyone I could tell, after— they all—died. I think—you'd listen—understand—"

"Yes, I will. I'm just going away for a minute to get you that soup. You stay quiet, you'll feel better when you've had that. Miss Riordan will be right here if you want anything." Her quick eye had brushed over Delia's ringless left hand. Competent and brisk, she went out.

Eileen lay quiet. After a minute she said, "You see, I never had a friend. Until Sharon. It was lonely after that—not having anybody."

And a minute later, "I felt—she was a friend. Marcella. And then I couldn't see her any more. I didn't know she was still there."

They helped her to sit up, and Marcella spooned most of the soup into her; she got a little color back. "Don't go," she said, and her eyes were pleading. "I want to tell you—I want to tell you how it all was—"

It all came out in a flood; she couldn't stop talking. Eileen didn't seem to know or care that Delia was still there; she kept her eyes on Marcella's face, talking, stopping, talking again.

The Dream— "I always knew it was waiting— Mrs. Gorman used to slap me for waking everybody up when I had it, but in Juvenile Hall they used to send me to a doctor—stupid, as if you could stop fate with a pill. Always exactly the same, the cat and what everybody said, and knowing I'd done something terribly wrong—" All the foster homes, and Social Services, and then the tremendous luck. And Mother Ruth.

Sharon, and Danny. "You can see I should have been with them. I would have been, half an hour later. Mrs. Redfern wouldn't even look at me. And I wasn't going to have Mother Ruth much longer— And nothing really mattered, I mean what happened to me— Knew there was something queer about it, it was just that I seemed to be in a kind of dream, because nothing mattered, I was going to be alone again—" Wesley. "Afterward, I thought—Mother Ruth didn't really mean that, that I should marry him—I don't think she did, now. But I thought so then, and she'd always taught me the right things to do— Are you still there?"

"I'm here. So you did. You weren't really thinking."

"No, I wasn't really thinking. I didn't want to be alone, but I was alone. Again. Because they didn't really want me. They only needed me—for the church." The rules set by the board of deacons. "I shouldn't have stayed. I don't know why I stayed. Yes, it was because I was stupid again. It was easier to try to forget it all—the library—all the books. I was alive when I was reading the books— and that time—talking with you. I was—I see that now—trying to run away. Wasn't I? And then—you see, there wasn't anyone else to *do* it. To take care of her. Do you know something funny, Marcella? It was a thought I had almost as soon as I found out about it—it

being all because of the church. They—we might have been talking
at each other in different languages. Never anything to say *to* each
other that meant anything."

"No, of course you hadn't. And after that, there was just the old
woman to take care of."

"Nobody else to do it. I hated her so much, you know, but I never
thought of killing her. You don't kill people. But it was all the time
—always getting me up at night, I suppose she couldn't help it, but
never saying thanks, sorry I disturbed— I wouldn't have minded if
I'd *liked* her— And so it happened. It just happened, I never meant
it. Just too much. That last time—and I had the scissors in my hand,
you see—the last I knew. I see now I have to pay, because of the
doom assigned."

In the silence, Marcella went on looking down at her for a long
moment, and reached to adjust the blanket. Eileen was sound asleep.
Marcella looked across at Delia on the other side of the bed, and
drew a long breath. They went out to the kitchen and sat at the little wooden table.

"Well!" said Marcella. "And it was past time all that came out of
her. All bottled up inside. That poor, poor child. I don't know about
you, but I could stand a good, stiff drink. Of course, there won't be a
drop in this place."

Delia got out cigarettes and offered them. They found a saucer to
use for an ashtray. "What do you think?" Delia asked.

"What do you?" countered Marcella. "I liked that child when I
first met her. She never told me much about her background—just
the bare fact about the foster homes. She seemed lost even then—"
She sighed. "I lost my husband three years ago—we never had any
children, and he didn't want to adopt—and well, I was interested in
her. Did you know she's got quite a little artistic talent? Do you
think," asked Marcella abruptly, "she stabbed that old woman?"

"No, I don't," said Delia. "I really don't, you know. I suppose
some people would say that girl was weak. I think, in a kind of way,
she's damned tough. She's been through this and that, but she hasn't
so much lain down under it as just gritted her teeth and stood it.
Which maybe takes more guts than lashing out in all directions at
fate when it can't get you anywhere."

"You're the lashing-out kind. So am I. But that's right," said Marcella. "What did she mean, 'the doom assigned'?"

"It's somewhere in Tennyson, I think. *The purpose of God and the doom assigned.*"

"Fate and free will," said Marcella.

"She never has lashed out before. In the technical phrase, shown any aggression. I just don't think it's in her. I think what happened is that all the buried resentment against the woman, against being trapped here, boiled up suddenly. She had to get away—so her conscious mind blacked out and she just went. God knows where. There's enough precedent for that kind of thing. And after a while she strayed home again, the subconscious telling her that was where she should be."

"You buy all the psychiatric doubletalk?"

"Not by a long way. Some of it." There had been instant rapprochement between them.

"And while she was gone, some character wandered in here and did the stabbing?"

"My current partner," said Delia, "has been telling me that it was always likelier it was the casual daylight burglar, panicked when he found somebody home. Now, he seems to buy her confession."

"Are they going to charge her?" asked Marcella.

"I don't know. There's a legal question. The husband's confessed too."

"For God's sake, why? That's ridiculous."

"Eileen says, being saintly. Trying to make up for his failures."

"I suppose that's likely. If they do charge her—she won't have a cent."

"He'll get his mother's money eventually. She had about a hundred thousand in mutual funds."

"Well, for the love of heaven!" said Marcella. "And working that girl to death— Well, there you *are*. Some people I know—even a twenty-year-old and not the lashing-out kind—would have said, you need a nurse, you can afford to hire one. But she just started in doing it, and I suppose after a while she was so worn out and short on sleep it was less trouble just to go on. Well, I'll guarantee a defense lawyer if they do charge her."

"I just wonder," said Delia slowly, "if we could prove she didn't do it."

"How on earth?"

"I don't know. Where did she go? When you knew her, were there any special places she liked to go?"

"The library," said Marcella dryly. "Which isn't open on Sunday, but would her subconscious mind know that? Forest Lawn of all places—she said it was so peaceful. Uptown to look at pictures at Aaron Brothers. I don't think she's ever been to a real art gallery in her life. I'd like to take her. She used to show me her drawings—there's real talent there, I think."

"She doesn't really know what time she went. She says she thinks some time after Wesley left for the Thrift Shop. Maybe two o'clock. He left about one. The estimated time of death is between one and two, but the doctor said there was a leeway."

"Well, I don't think she did it either," said Marcella. "You heard what she said—you don't kill people. She hasn't got it in her. And if it looks funny that she certainly had some provocation, and blacked out like that and ran away, and then somebody did come in and kill the woman—well, it'll just have to look funny. And you know the sole reason she's convinced she did kill her is that damned dream."

"Which is funny in itself," said Delia. "I don't know that I quite buy that dream."

"You don't believe in recurring dreams?"

"Ask me if I believe tomorrow's Saturday. They happen. Oftener than you might think. And predictive ones, too. But there are some funny things about that dream."

Marcella waited, and when she didn't enlarge on that, said, "Well, somebody's got to look after her. I'd like to get her to a doctor, she's run-down and very likely anemic. This place—I'd like to take her to my home. Is that all right?"

"If you let us have the address. He's going to lose this church, you know, and they couldn't stay here anyway."

"They!" said Marcella. "I'm not an advocate of divorce, but sometimes you have to cut losses. She hasn't any reason to stay tied to that—"

"Piece of chewed string," said Delia. "That's another example. She should have cut and run, and she didn't."

"Oh, she was running—she sees that now, she said so. Pretending it hadn't happened. When do you think we'll know if they are going to arrest her?"

"I haven't the slightest idea," said Delia. "O'Connor'll be fit to be tied. The supermale tough cop—he doesn't like loose ends, and the DA doesn't like to waste taxpayers' money. Hah! Talk about sick jokes."

Marcella scribbled an address and phone number on a memo sheet from her bag. "Well, that's where we'll be. You'll let me know what goes on."

———◆———

O'Connor was annoyed, but also amused. He got hold of an assistant DA who was more than annoyed at being disturbed on Saturday, but agreed to come in for an hour. "And I hope to hell they decide to leave it alone," said O'Connor. "What a goddamned tangle! If they do decide to charge her, we'll come in for more legwork trying to prove he couldn't have done it—not that anybody could believe he did. Who in hell commits sympathetic euthanasia with a pair of scissors? But juries can be convinced of almost any goddamned thing. Try to trace him back, when he got on the bus, etc.—with the time of death so elastic? Oh, I agree with you, Vic—she did it all right, it all fits. God knows she probably had reason to fly off the handle at that old bitch. But I don't think—also considering the convenient amnesia—the DA's going to like it, as a case."

The assistant DA didn't either. He said it was an interesting situation, legally, but unless the picture should change, any physical evidence turn up, it would be unlikely they'd get a conviction. Psychiatrists' opinions really broken reeds, just opinions, try to prove or disprove the amnesia. Even if the first confession could be shown to be false, a defense attorney—and juries— Even if they did decide to bring a charge, there would probably be plea bargaining, a reduced charge—manslaughter with diminished responsibility— He would have to put it to the DA on Monday, see what his recommendation might be.

"Doubletalk!" said O'Connor when he'd gone. "He knows as well as we do it'd be a damn waste of time. But how often are we morally sure that somebody did something, and can't prove it all legal by the book? I hope they decide to leave it lay, but if they don't, at least it's their baby, off our hands."

Which were still busy.

By now, they knew that those prints out of the Jensen house weren't in anybody's records. They were still looking for the latest heist man, and for the burglar, but that would go in Pending, no leads at all. Eustace would be arraigned on Monday; Echeverria had been arraigned on Friday, and presently somebody would have to cover both indictments.

On Saturday night there were two more heists and another burglary.

On Sunday afternoon, just in case the DA decided to go out on a limb, which they strongly doubted, Varallo went down to that Thrift Shop on Colorado. It was run by the Disabled Veterans; the volunteer there seemed reasonably efficient. Yes, she was here every Sunday, she said. Asked to cast her mind back two weeks ago, she gave Varallo a little surprise. Oh yes, she remembered the man who'd come in looking for curtains; he had asked to borrow a yardstick. And she knew the time, definitely. It was a quarter to one.

"Are you sure?" Varallo was taken aback.

"Oh yes. There's a little sermonette on the local radio station I always listen to, and he'd been in the store a minute or two when it came on. It was just a minute after that he'd asked for the yardstick."

In one way, it was helpful; rather definitely it put Wesley out of the running, and it wasn't surprising he should be vague about time.

He got back to the station just as the traffic shift was changing at four o'clock, and found Katz talking to a crowd of uniformed men in the lobby.

He passed that on to O'Connor, who had dropped in on his day off to see what was going on, and O'Connor said, "Well, that takes him off the hook. They might decide to take her in for it at that."

Katz came in five minutes later. "What was the gathering with traffic about?" asked Varallo. "Reclaiming your lost youth, or what?"

"Or what," said Katz. "Tell me I'm an idiot when the brainwave doesn't pay off. There's a new moon tomorrow night, and the area isn't all that big."

CHAPTER 9

"He was there that early?" asked Delia in surprise. Everyone else was out on something, just after eight on Monday morning; she'd walked in to hear Varallo talking to O'Connor.

"Yes, it takes him off the hook. I'd better call the DA's office and let them know," said O'Connor.

"But if that's so," said Delia, "then there was time. Eileen doesn't really know what time she blacked out, only that it was after he'd left. It could have been just after. She could have been gone from the house by one o'clock, and that leaves time for someone else—"

"Oh, lady," said Varallo, "don't reach."

"Beating a dead horse," said O'Connor, irritated. "It's off our hands. If the DA decides to try to nail her for it, they'll let us know, and we go pick her up and bring her in and that's that. Meanwhile, there's a hell of a lot of other things to do."

"Emotions," said Varallo, and shook his head at her.

Quite suddenly Delia lost her temper, which she did in a dangerously quiet way. She stood up and said to both of them, "Every detective I've ever known, and it may surprise you to hear that I've known a few, tells me that any good detective gets gut feelings about cases—about the people in cases. Well, I've got a gut feeling about that girl. And I'll remind you, Lieutenant, that it's not out of our hands—technically the investigation is still open, nobody's been arrested and charged. And I think I'd like to do a little more investigating on it." She picked up her bag and walked out, leaving them staring after her.

The main office of the Southern California Rapid Transit Company was in downtown LA. It would probably be quicker and save trouble to go than try it by phone. She looked up the address in the phone book in the lobby, and took the freeway. It was Broadway; she left the Mercedes in a lot up the street and walked back, picked up a valley bus schedule from the main desk, and showed the badge. The badge was very helpful, opening doors and getting questions answered. In due time she got an official who could tell her what she wanted to know.

According to the Sunday schedule, there was really only one bus Wesley could have taken. The No. 4 went up Brand to Broadway, turned there; he'd have gotten off at Jackson and walked two blocks down to that Thrift Shop. The schedule only listed main intersections, but the bus was due at Broadway and Brand at twelve thirty-five, and there wasn't another No. 4 before it since eleven-fifteen or another after it until one-fifty.

She wanted to get hold of the driver. The official was co-operative and curious; it took a little while, but he chased it down for her. The driver was Bill Lang, he was off today, and he had an address in the Atwater district.

Delia found it: Madera Avenue. Bill Lang was home, with his wife and three noisy kids, and he looked startled at the badge. "Look," he said, "I wouldn't remember any passengers. They get to be just faces, you don't really see them. They got to have exact change now, you know, on account of so many holdups, it's only if they want a transfer ticket I even speak to 'em."

"Yes, I know. But can you tell me if you were on schedule that Sunday? Two weeks ago yesterday?"

"Lady," he said, "Sundays I'm always on schedule. I'm drivin' around with half the seats empty most weekdays, but Sundays there's hardly anybody, and not near so much traffic. Sure I was on schedule."

"You were due at Broadway and Brand at twelve thirty-five. When would you hit Brand and Chevy Chase?"

"Couldn't be much off twelve-thirty, it's hardly a four-five-minute run."

"And Broadway and Jackson?"

"Call it twelve thirty-eight to twelve-forty. What's this all about, anyway?"

"To settle a bet," said Delia. "Thanks very much."

Somebody had said—Mr. Dudey—that with attendance at the church dropping, the congregation didn't tend to linger around talking after the service, it dispersed right away. That would fit in.

She drove back to Glendale and found Marcella Moore's address on California Street. It was an unpretentious old place, a big old California bungalow painted white with green trim, behind a green lawn and rose bushes.

Eileen looked better already, but her eyes on Delia were briefly alarmed and then resigned. "No, I haven't come to arrest you. I've got some questions for you," said Delia. It was a comfortably furnished long living room with an old oriental carpet, one wall lined with bookshelves.

"I think," said Eileen, "that you're both crazy. Marcella's been telling me. It's very—well, kind of you to think I didn't do it, but we all know I did. I couldn't understand why you didn't arrest me, and then Marcella told me—Wesley—being so silly like that, so it would be confusing."

Marcella said, "I was just going to fix some lunch—it's nearly twelve. Would you like some?"

"I certainly would," said Delia. "I didn't have much breakfast. Thanks." Marcella vanished into the kitchen.

"I've told her she shouldn't be doing all this for me. I'm nobody of hers. But she's so good—I don't deserve it."

"Tosh," said Marcella, looking in again. "Do you take cream and sugar? It's not as if I can't afford to keep the shop closed another week."

Over lunch, Delia put the question to Eileen. "I don't know," said Eileen. "I told you I haven't been wearing a watch. Was it that early? It could have been, I suppose. People hadn't been staying, after church. Wesley said he didn't want any lunch. But—I had the feeling that it was *a while* later, at least—" She sighed. "I'd been measuring for those curtains— I hate sewing so. I don't know what time it was, honestly."

"I see it could make a difference," said Marcella. "All that more leeway."

"It doesn't make any difference at all," said Eileen. "Or whether I remember it or not. Because I know I must have done it. The

Dream really predicted it. I couldn't *not* have done it." She was looking tired again.

"There is such a thing as free will," said Marcella.

"All the time?" said Eileen. "I think the Dream had to happen in real life—it was like fate. And you know, Marcella, if that's true— about the law of karma— I'd rather pay for it now, for the wrong, and not have it—hanging over me."

"Yes, well," said Delia, "I've got another idea too. We'll see how that works out. And as far as the Dream goes—"

"You don't believe it," said Eileen.

"Let's say I don't put much faith in recurring dreams as solid evidence," said Delia dryly.

As she went down the cement walk to the car, she noticed a cat crouched on the porch of the neighboring house: a fat gray cat calmly and sleepily watching the passing scene with the complacent blandness of all cats.

⟶◆⟵

She had just gotten back to the office when a new call came in from the security guards at The Broadway, one of the department stores in the Galleria shopping mall. She went out on it with Varallo.

"First time we knew you could be a spitfire," he said in the Gremlin.

"I'm not really. Was the lieutenant mad?"

"Charles? Mad at anybody for blowing off steam? But you're butting your head on a stone wall. It's a waste of time—even if they charge her, it'd be a minimum term."

"Which would be too much if she's not guilty," said Delia.

At The Broadway, the security guards were holding three people. The man had grudgingly parted with names, no more: Lorenzo Guttierez, Lucia Guttierez, Maria. Maria looked about twelve. "They were on their third trip when we collared them," said the chief guard. "They've got a van in the lot. I ask you, my God, walk in with a shopping bag, stuff it full of clothes off the rack, and walk out—"

The van was full of miscellaneous merchandise, all new and still tagged: mostly clothes, some small appliances, pots and pans, curtain rods, sheets and blankets, all sorts of stuff. This was just the latest caper of a kind getting more and more common in Southern California, the wholesale shoplifting to order for relaying to the black market across the Mexican border. Most of it was just as brazen as this; security guards couldn't be everywhere, and during busy hours neither could the salesclerks.

They called up a squad car to ferry them in, and the garage to come and tow in the van. They tried to talk to the Guttierezes. The parents made out that they couldn't speak any English, but were given away by Maria's coming out with some choice Anglo-Saxon terms for the dirty cops. Suppressing a grin, Varallo asked for identification. "Naturalization papers? Citizens?"

"No se."

"——cops," said Maria succinctly.

"Address? Where you live? Er, *indirizzo*?" said Varallo.

"I don't think it's the same in Spanish," said Delia. "Try *dirección*."

"No *se*," said Guttierez with a scowl. His wife wept.

"Dirty stinking pigs," said Maria.

There was a receipt for a motel room on Guttierez, a cheap place on the outskirts of town. It was practically a foregone conclusion that they were illegal aliens, so Varallo called Immigration, and a couple of officers came over.

"Well, Lorenzo," said the first one in, "you back again? Got the family with you this time, hah? Many hands make light work."

"Damn it," said the other one, "this is getting to be too much of a good thing. God knows how many of these damned wetbacks are getting ferried over here to supply that black-market ring in Mexico. All we can do is charge them, and they jump bail, or get turned loose by the court and we dump 'em over the border, and I swear to God we're not out of sight before they head North again." Maria said what she thought of him, and he looked startled. But they took them off Glendale's hands, and there'd just be the paperwork on it.

Poor was off today, but the rest had been in and out with the possible suspects. Paul Jensen's brother had come in on Saturday and was still here; he showed up to talk to O'Connor.

Delia typed the report on the Guttierezes; as she ripped the triple form out of the machine, Varallo said, "I'd like to know how your mind's working, on that Endicott girl."

"If anything ever comes of it I'll tell you," said Delia. "We haven't heard anything from the DA's office."

"Maybe they're still mulling it over."

"Well, it'll be interesting to see what they decide to do," said Delia. She slapped the cover on the typewriter and got up. "See you in the morning."

As she came past O'Connor's desk, he was complaining to Katz, "It's not natural, damn it. All this physical evidence, and it doesn't give us any damn direction to go."

"At least be grateful for small favors," said Katz. "You're catching up on your sleep."

It had turned colder again, and as she got out the car keys, Delia looked hopefully into a gray sky. They needed rain: another dry winter. The six-o'clock traffic was getting thick, but she made fairly good time through town, heading toward Hollywood down Riverside to Los Feliz. Just after the intersection where three main drags came together she slid out of traffic to the side street off Los Feliz, and a minute later turned the Mercedes into the drive of the rambling old Spanish two-story stucco on Waverly Place.

She came in the back door. There was a fine smell in the kitchen: lasagna in the oven, bread all cut for cheese toast, asparagus steaming, a generous pot of hollandaise sauce. That probably meant the rich spice cakes and rum sauce for dessert, which she'd better not have. She went down the hall and paused on the threshold; they hadn't heard her come in, and were sitting there in companionable silence, one of them reading *Master Detective* and the other one *True Detective*.

Alex Riordan, losing his first wife after twenty years of childless marriage, had married a girl half his age, only to lose her in childbirth a year later. They had managed, he and Delia, somehow, with a succession of housekeepers, until that year Delia was thirteen and he was sixty-five. He'd been full of excited plans for her first time of entering the junior target pistol competitions—he'd started her with a gun on her seventh birthday. Then, just two days before his official retirement, he'd gone out on his last call— Captain Alex Riordan, Robbery-Homicide, LAPD—and taken the bank robber's slug in the spine. That had been a bad time, for a while, and then they had found Steve. Ex-Sergeant Steve McAllister, LAPD, retired, just short of twenty-five years' service when he'd lost a leg in an accident: a widower with a married daughter in Denver. The three of them had been together for thirteen years now. The new leg didn't hamper Steve from maneuvering the wheelchair, and Alex had always liked to cook.

"You're late," said Steve, looking up. "Something break on that Jensen case?"

"It'll go in Pending." Delia took his chair as he got up to start the toast. "Alex, do we know any hypnotists?"

He cocked his handsome head at her, his mane of white hair a little untidy. Oh, of course, of course, it had had to be this job, for Alex. "What the hell do you want with a hypnotist?" She told him, and he scratched his chin thoughtfully. "Not admissible evidence, of course. But it might be interesting. Got a lot of contacts among us, we should be able to locate one. You really think that girl didn't do it?"

"Gut feeling."

"Well, I always taught you not to worry about consequences when you're sure you're right. Come on, that toast will be ready, and the lasagna's just right."

———◆———

At 1 A.M. on Monday night, with a sharp new sickle of moon sailing high in the sky, Patrolman Gordon, slowly cruising up Olmstead Drive, spotted what looked like a prowler sneaking down a driveway in the middle of the block. He curbed the car silently, got out, easing his door shut, loosening the gun in the holster. He expected the prowler to cut and run any second, when he spotted the black-and-white, but the figure came on openly down the drive to the sidewalk, walking along as if it were the middle of the day. It was carrying something in one hand, a tool, a gun.

"Hold it, buddy!" snapped Gordon. The figure kept right on going, as if it hadn't heard. As it came under a street light, Gordon saw that it was just a kid, a teen-ager. Gordon loped up behind and grabbed him. "I said hold it! Don't make a move—drop what you're holding!" It was a great big wrench. The kid didn't make any effort to get away, just stood there. And he was wearing pajamas and bedroom slippers, nothing else. Gordon took his arm roughly to get him over to the car, and all of a sudden the kid gave a convulsive leap, and yelled, and started to shake all over.

"What—" he said. "Where—how did I get here, what are you—"

"Here, take it easy," said Gordon, somewhat alarmed. He got the kid into the car and called a backup, who turned out to be Morris. By the time they got to the station the kid had told them his name and asked for his parents.

They went back to Olmstead and woke up the householder, and looking, found the windshield smashed on the Nova in the garage. The big door of the garage had been locked, not the little one.

"By God," said Gordon to Morris, "it looks as if Katz hit the target all right. But what a damned funny thing!"

———◄◆►———

Over Monday night there was an armed robbery on the street outside an all-night restaurant on South Brand. The middle-aged couple who'd been held up couldn't say much about the bandit except that he was young and had long hair. They'd be in to make a statement. Unexpectedly, the tape recorder that was part of the loot from the Goodman burglary turned up at a pawn shop in Burbank, and Varallo chased over to find out who'd pawned it. All the pawnbroker could tell him was a young fellow he'd never seen before, and so what if it was a couple days ago? "Look, I'm alone in this place, and I'm still trying to get used to these damn bifocals. Do I sit down every day and check over all the serial numbers of everything on the hot list? I never got burned before. I gave him twenty bucks for it, it cost a hundred new, and it's practically new." He produced the carbon of the signed form: The signature looked like Carlos Fortuna, an address on Milford.

Varallo came back to Glendale and found that. It was a solid old four-family place. Fortuna was listed in the top left.

"Sure, he's here," said the fat middle-aged woman who answered the door. And then when he produced the badge, she looked frightened. "A cop—what's it about? We haven't done nothing, we're honest people— Carlos, it's a cop, you better come—"

"A cop?" The young fellow across the shabby neat living room looked more surprised than scared. He got up and said, "Come in. What you want?"

"You pawned a tape recorder a couple of days ago, over in Burbank."

"Yeah, that's right. I work over there, it was the handiest place to the job. Now, Mama, stop fussing. Cops don't arrest honest people, and I haven't done anything wrong. I'm on nights with Lee's Towing on Hollywood Way. What's with the tape recorder?"

"It was stolen. Part of a burglary."

"You don't say! I'll be damned. I never thought anything about it," said Fortuna. "This guy owed me fifteen bucks for quite a while, and I'd sort of kissed it good-bye. I was real surprised when he came by the shop and asked me would I take the recorder and call it quits. It looked like a pretty good one—not that I know much about the things—so I said OK. And I got twenty bucks for it. What use have I got for a tape recorder?"

"Who's the guy? Work with you?"

"Nope. He used to be the short-order cook at this place a lot of us drop in for late snacks. Bella's on Victory Boulevard. He got in a bind a while back: his wife just had a baby, and they were behind on the rent. Look, I know how that goes, I remember how tight it was when Lola had the first one, I let him have the dough. He seemed like a nice enough guy." He looked at Varallo doubtfully. "Am I going to be in trouble on account of it?"

"Not when you didn't know it was stolen property. What's his name?"

"Sam Guardino. I don't know where's he's working now. Bella got in a bind too and had to let him go. I never did know where he lives."

It had, at last, begun to rain. Varallo found the restaurant on Victory Boulevard, but it didn't open until 2 P.M. Frustrated, he went back to the office.

Katz came in just after he did and told them about the moon-struck vandal. "It's the funniest damn thing I ever came across. I'd told the boys to try to keep that area covered better than usual, just on the chance. I know we said the moon sets some people off, but they're usually more or less aware of what they're doing, if not why. This one wasn't. He's a nice kid, Tim Meriweather, nice home, nice parents. They're all upset as hell. Nobody had any idea he'd taken to sleepwalking."

"Sleepwalking!" said O'Connor. "I will be goddamned! You mean he didn't know he was going out smashing up the cars?"

"No idea. He says he was never so scared in his life when he woke up all of a sudden and found himself out on the street with a police-man holding onto him." Katz laughed. "It sounds crazy, but the doc-tor said it happens oftener than you might think. I mean their doc-tor—old-fashioned family doctor too, he came out right away when they called. Gordon got me out of bed because he knew I'd be inter-ested."

"That's the queerest one we've had in a while," agreed Varallo. "Why was he doing it? I don't mean sleepwalking, I mean smashing up the cars."

"Well, I expect six head-doctors would give you six answers," said Katz. "I never saw a kid so—so flabbergasted when we told him, when he realized what he'd been doing. Kept saying, gee, he'd never do a thing like that in his right mind, was he going crazy or some-thing. But we came to some kind of conclusion, the parents and the doctor and me. Like all sixteen-year-olds he's crazy to have a car of his own, and he's got a learner's permit, he's allowed to drive the family car sometimes with his mother or father along. But Meri-weather's a solid, sensible citizen, and he lays down the rule that if Tim wants a car he'll get a job and pay for it himself. So it'll proba-bly be a good long time before Tim gets a car, and meanwhile there must have been some resentment and envy bottled up. The Meri-weathers live on Norton, by the way—right in the middle of the area."

"Comes the change of the moon," said O'Connor, "Tim's subcon-scious mind sent him out sleepwalking to smash up other people's cars? Be damned."

"That seems to be about it. It's funny, you wouldn't think in that state he'd be able to open and shut doors—even unlocked doors—or, for that matter, find his way home again and be tucked up safe in bed the next morning. But the doctor said they do queerer things than that."

"What's going to happen to him?" asked Delia.

Katz shrugged. "He's under age. Even if he'd known he was doing it, it'd be a year's probation. Most of the damage was covered by insurance. I think he was more horrified than the owners were. He says gee, they better lock him in every night and put bars on the windows. The doctor said possibly the shock of finding out about it might stop it. At any rate, they'll keep an eye on him from now on."

"And as I've been saying," said O'Connor, losing interest in Tim, "this Jensen thing is damned frustrating. Goddamned frustrating. All that physical evidence, and it all goes to a dead end. Nobody knows those prints. Blond hairs in the damned hat, if that's what you call it—big deal!" He had the hat on his desk; apparently the lab was finished with it. "It's easy enough to reconstruct what must have happened. Jensen was a recluse, as they say, but he did answer his doorbell. Witness the neighbor with the petition. He answered the doorbell, probably at night, and they pushed in to find his money. Ended up knifing him either because they didn't find much or because that's just the kind they are. And brother Bill, not very close, hadn't seen him in ten years, can't tell us about anything maybe missing from the house. The only thing he does tell us is that Paul had a watch, not new but a very fine solid gold watch, a Gerard-Perrigaux. Naturally, he doesn't know the serial number. And goddamn it, that's all, and it takes us nowhere. There's no damn handle."

"That's the hat you've been talking about?" asked Delia. "From the Jensen place? Well, I can give you some idea about that." She reached over and picked it up. "It's not a hat, it's a hand-knitted beret, and it isn't something that anybody over about twenty would be likely to wear. Not this year." She pulled out the big pompon on top, the long, tangled string from the middle of it ending in a fat tassel. The whole thing was striped in a rash of different garish colors: red, yellow, green, purple, royal blue. "There's a fashion for these things with the teen-agers right now. You see them on kids all over."

"Is that so?" said O'Connor. "Seems you're some use around here after all. But if you can tell me anywhere that suggests to look—"

"The neighborhood, the neighborhood," said Varallo. "Where the rumor passed that he was a miser. God knows we see a lot of the unnecessary violence these days, from all sorts and ages, but the edge is on the young ones."

"Somebody," said Delia, "might recognize this, you know."

"*E vero*," said Varallo thoughtfully. "That's so. Which is today's great thought. You've earned your pay for the week."

"Anything in from the DA's office?" she asked O'Connor, and he shook his head absently.

The desk buzzed. "You've got an attempted homicide," said Duff. "Randolph Street."

When Varallo and Delia got there, it wasn't exactly an attempted homicide; that had been Mrs. Brice's first excited report: "Somebody's tried to kill my husband!" By the time the detectives got there, Patrolman Stoner had helped him up off the floor, and he was sitting in a chair holding an ice bag to his head and saying he was all right.

"Damn it, you expect burglars in the middle of the night! Glendale used to be a nice quiet town, low crime rate—damn it, Martha, stop fussing, it was just a knock on the head." He looked a little blearily at the detectives. "Sitting here reading the paper while Martha's out at the market—sitting here quiet in my own house! I go out to the kitchen for a glass of water, there's a damn burglar in the bedroom, pawing through drawers! In broad daylight! Well, of course the doors weren't locked, I was right there. Would I lock Martha out, she comes home with a hundred bucks' worth of groceries? And the bastard comes at me with a club or something; it all happened so fast I couldn't see—"

"Can you give us any description of him, sir?"

"That I can, sort of. He was a Latin of some kind, dark, with a little mustache. Early twenties, I guess. Medium height, thin."

"Which is more than we sometimes get," said Varallo back in the car. He was debating whether it would be any use to get Burt out to dust for prints. Probably not.

"It could even," said Delia, "be Esteban Garcia."

He stared at her. "Today's second great thought."

When the traffic shift was due to change at four o'clock, she went down to the parking lot in back of the jail, and caught Tracy and Fenner just coming on. "I've got some questions for you. Mind taking a few minutes?"

"Sure. What about?" asked Tracy. Their two cars were side by side in the lot; they all got into Tracy's, Delia in the back, out of the thin rain.

"The day you got called to the body on Elm Street. Two weeks ago Sunday. I want you to think back to when the girl—young Mrs. Endicott—came in."

"OK. What about it?" asked Tracy. "I was there first. I called for a backup and the detectives, and the girl came in just before Bill got there."

"Try to remember just what was said—well, what you said. Did you say to either of them, 'It was deliberate murder'?"

Tracy stared at her, his young bulldog face puzzled. "Not very likely I'd say that. Not exactly—well, the jargon we use, is it? If I'd said anything—well, yes, I did say to Endicott that it was homicide."

"Yes," said Delia. "Did you say, 'There's nothing you can do for her now'?"

"Yes, I think I said that to the girl. She was going over to that wheelchair, and the corpse wasn't a very nice sight, I didn't want her to—"

"Very natural," said Delia. "A thing anybody might have said. Did either of you say, 'We'll have to leave that to the detectives'?"

"Leave what?" said Fenner. "No. What I did say—no, I guess it was Neil—Endicott was fidgeting around and asking what were we doing, weren't we doing anything, and Neil naturally said, 'We have to wait for the detectives.' What's this about?"

"And who said, 'I don't know why it had to happen!'?"

They looked at each other and shrugged. "Endicott—or the girl, I guess," said Tracy. "It's the kind of thing people do say at a time like that."

"So it is," said Delia. She thought for a minute and then asked, "Was the cat there when you first went in?"

"Yes, it was," said Tracy. "I remember noticing that—sitting on the back of a chair. Big gray cat."

"Well, thanks," said Delia. "I can't tell you what it's all about because I'm not at all sure myself."

She went out of her way to stop at the house on California. By the smell from the kitchen, Marcella had a pot roast in the oven

They were both intrigued, and raised no objections. "It might just do the trick," said Marcella. "Be interesting to try, if Eileen doesn't mind."

"Oh, I wouldn't mind. And—if it did make me tell, it couldn't be any worse than it is now. I mean, if I came right out and said I did it, if I remembered it then, it wouldn't be any different for me because I know I did."

"What about the DA?" asked Marcella.

"Nothing. You understand, whichever way it goes, this wouldn't be admissible evidence at a trial."

"So we've got nothing to lose. And maybe something to gain. If Eileen's game, I am. You've got somebody lined up? Is he good?"

"Supposed to be. Of course, it depends on how good a subject you turn out to be," said Delia to Eileen. "Some people can't be, but I understand relatively few."

"I'd like to try." Eileen smiled at her. "I saw Marcella's doctor today, and he says it's no wonder I've been tired and my mind maybe not working the way it should—my blood count's way down, and so is my blood pressure. I've got to rest, and he gave me some vitamins. I suppose it's no good looking for a job until we know if I'm going to jail."

"No good at all," said Marcella. "And if you don't go to jail you can pay me back all the room and board after you've got a job." She came out on the porch with Delia and said, "I'm keeping my fingers crossed about the DA."

"So am I. But even if they decide to let it lay, she's convinced she did it."

"Look," said Marcella forthrightly, "even if they do charge her, it wouldn't be a long term—two, three years. She's young. She damn well deserves something out of life, more than she's had. I'm going to see she gets it. And if they don't—well, she can get a job, pay me room and board if she insists—which she would—and we'll see about some art lessons on the side. And she'll get shut of that dim-witted minister and with any luck someday she'll meet a real man to love her and take care of her."

"Happy ever after," said Delia. "You've appointed yourself her guardian angel, anyhow."

"Tosh," said Marcella, looking amused. "Give me an interest in life."

"Look hard at the door," said Dr. Wagner in his quiet, soothing voice. "You are going through it in just a minute. You are very drowsy. You can't keep your eyes open. You can hear only my voice, and you will answer me. There is the door in front of you. You are going through it now. Now. Now. Do you see the door opening?"

The contacts had turned up Dr. Wagner. He was unexpectedly young, with what Alex called a checkered record: impeccable degrees, a staff psychiatrist position at UCLA Medical Center, and association with several parapsychological research organizations. Delia had spent an hour with him in his office this afternoon, and he knew just what they were after.

He had been unexpectedly quick, too. He couldn't have been here half an hour. "If you're a middling good subject," he'd said, smiling at Eileen. "Snap, it'll be done. No problem. Everything's always there in your subconscious mind—you just have to reach for it."

And now he was saying, "Through the door. It's open, and you've gone through. You hear me and will answer me. You've gone back to the moment when you are standing in the bedroom. It's Sunday, the church services are over, and your husband has left. You are thinking about making curtains. You are there. Tell me you are there."

"Yes," said Eileen. She was lying back in the deep upholstered armchair in Marcella's living room. It was eight o'clock on Wednesday night. Her eyes were barely half open. "Yes, I'm there."

"You are going to see everything that happens from now on. I want you to tell me about it, as it happens."

"I am cutting the curtains. She calls—hurts my head—my head—Eileen, I want you! She always calls that way, I can't stand it—I—have—to—get away. I can't—any more—it's too much—" Her thin breast heaved; she was gasping. Marcella and Delia leaned forward.

"It's all right—you are free of that now, it cannot trouble you. You are seeing yourself at that moment. How long is it since your husband left the house?"

"I don't know. I don't know."

"All right. Tell me what is happening. She called you. What is happening?"

"I can't I can't I can't," said Eileen. "I am coming out of the bedroom. I throw the scissors at her, they fall in her lap, she looks so surprised—funny—she never thought I'd do that. I have to get away, and I am going out. I'm walking up the street. There's a bus coming up to the corner."

Delia thought sharply, now, which one? It all depended on the time—the time. If it was the one immediately after Bill Lang's bus, the one due to go straight up Brand and turn on Kenneth to go to Burbank—that would have been barely ten minutes later.

"I am getting on the bus. I have my change purse in my sweater pocket, for the collection at church. There are only two other people on the bus; I don't notice them much, I can't see what they look like. I'm getting off the bus, I'm going across the street to look at the pictures—the pictures in the store windows on the corner."

Aaron Brothers at Broadway and Brand.

"That's fine. Go on telling me what's happening."

"There's a woman—on the bench at the corner—she's a colored woman, she's thin and tall. She's got on a black coat and a blue scarf. She's a nice woman—you can see it in her face—she's kind—

and she's sad. She's talking to another woman there—nobody else around—she's asking what bus to take to get to Forest Lawn." Suddenly Eileen laughed a delighted little laugh. "I can't help it, it's such a funny name! She's telling the woman—they've got to talking, I can hear everything—she's saying she wants to go and pay her respects—such a funny idea when the person's not there at all, only a shell—and how she didn't know she'd died, such a nice lady, she'd worked for her twenty years—such a funny name, Mrs. Blossom Penray. She's been back East visiting her daughter, and when she came home, her husband told her Mrs. Penray had died. The other woman's telling her, 'the Hollywood bus, and you have to walk down'—"

"That's fine. What are you doing?"

"I hadn't—thought about it—in so long. Where it's so beautiful. The swans. I'm getting on the bus with her. The nice colored lady. I don't speak to her, we're just on the bus together. We get off and walk down. The gates are open—the gates are always open. I am going in, over to sit on the bench by the pond where the swans are."

"The other woman," said Delia quietly.

"Where does the colored woman go?"

"I don't know. Yes, she went into the building there—across the road." Eileen began to moan and move a little. "But I shouldn't be here—I shouldn't have gone away—I ought to go back. I don't want to go back, but I have to."

"All right. Do you know what time it is?"

"No, but late—it's cold. I've been here too long, I have to go back. I am getting up—starting to walk back—"

"All right." Dr. Wagner gave a quick look at Delia. "Now you are going to wake and feel fine, Eileen. You will wake when I count three, and you will feel fine, and you will remember everything you have told me. You will remember everything. Now you will wake, and remember. One, two, three."

Eileen was silent, but her eyes opened naturally. After a moment she said disappointedly, looking at the doctor, "It didn't work. You said it worked with most people, but it didn't."

"On the contrary," said Dr. Wagner, smiling, "it worked fine."

"And you didn't," said Marcella excitedly. "I knew you didn't. You said—"

Eileen looked at them blankly. "What did I say? I don't remember a thing."

"But you gave her a posthypnotic suggestion—she ought to remember!" Marcella turned to Dr. Wagner.

He shook his head. "It's very unusual. Occasionally it happens. There may be a block of some kind there."

"But you said you didn't do it, darling," said Marcella. "You just threw the scissors at her, you said—"

"And killed her. What does it matter what I said? I'd be lying—not wanting to pay for it—"

———◆———

The ward nurse was young and efficient, knowing her job. She settled down all her patients for the night, competently, and returned to the ward station, keeping her eye out for lighted-up bells showing on the board. The second traction patient in Ward 4 asked for a urinal at two-thirty, but she never glanced at the patient in the next bed; he seemed to be sleeping soundly.

The man in the next bed to Wesley Endicott had left a pair of nail scissors on the table between the beds, and at some time after midnight Wesley had used them quietly to cut both the veins in his wrists. His arms were under the blankets, so it wasn't discovered until the change of shift at 7 A.M., and then it was too late.

"You can't blame me," was the night nurse's automatic reaction, defensive, shocked. "Doctor, honestly, he was—you can't blame me! I thought I'd finally convinced him he wasn't going to die!"

CHAPTER 10

That was the first thing they heard on Thursday morning: the hospital report. "Well, for God's sake!" said O'Connor. "Wouldn't you know that's just what he'd do, that little twerp, for no reason at all—"

"I expect he thought he had one," said Delia.

"—Just confusing everything worse. That about puts the damn lid on it— I'll bet the DA wouldn't touch that case with a ten-foot pole. And I wouldn't give a damn, but I don't like loose ends, I don't like to see a case die on the vine like this."

Varallo and Forbes were still hunting for Guardino; there'd been another armed robbery on the street last night, sounding much like the other one, and Poor was out on that. Delia called Marcella before she left the office, and Marcella echoed O'Connor.

"Yes, of course the hospital called. And isn't it just the sort of miserable end that idiot would make! For no reason at all. Oh, Eileen's taking it all right, it's not as if he ever meant much to her—or vice versa!—she said poor Wesley just couldn't cope with life, which God knows seems to be the truth. We'll be going out later to arrange things. At least she knows which lawyer he went to about his mother's will, but when he didn't leave one I suppose the state will grab two thirds of his miserable bank account. No, I'm not feeling charitable toward the man," said Marcella frankly. "But we're coping."

O'Connor had gone out. Delia left the office empty and embarked on her bloodhounding project for the day. She wasn't any too hopeful of getting anywhere, but as a matter of fact it turned out to be absurdly simple.

"The building across the road" from the pond and the swans at Forest Lawn was, of course, the business office. The badge produced courteous co-operation, and they kept excellent records. Mrs. Blossom Penray had been interred on Sunset Slope just five weeks ago. The arrangements had been made by her husband, Mr. Howard Penray, an address on Kenneth Road in Glendale.

It was one of the old dignified two-story English houses built long before taxes began to soar. There was a FOR SALE sign on the lawn in front. Not expecting an answer, Delia pushed the bell; but Mr. Penray was there. He looked at the badge, and heard her question with some surprise.

"Why, that would be Rachel," he said. "Rachel Penny. She's worked for us for years. Every Monday, Wednesday, and Friday." He was a tall, stoop-shouldered old man. "She was quite distressed about it—she'd been back in Illinois visiting her daughter when it happened, it was quite sudden, you see—a coronary attack. But what do the police want with Rachel?"

"She's a possible witness to something," said Delia. "Could you give me her address?"

"Why, certainly." He looked frail and ill; he didn't ask any more questions. "I think she'll be home—this had been her only job for some time, her family didn't like her working so hard any more. I'm sure you'll find her co-operative"—he gave Delia an absent smile—"her son is a patrolman with the LAPD."

It was an address in Hollywood: Rosewood Avenue off Vermont, a narrow old street of modest old frame houses, but all neatly enough maintained. The one she wanted was freshly painted yellow with white trim. Mrs. Rachel Penny peered at the badge and welcomed her into a neat, well-furnished living room. "What's it about?"

"You took a bus over to Glendale two weeks ago last Sunday," said Delia. She sat down at the gesture of invitation.

"Why, yes, I did. I'd have gotten Jim, my boy, to drive me, but he's on duty Sundays. I just felt I couldn't let it go." Mrs. Penny paused, but Delia's encouraging silence sent her on. "You see, it was a terrible shock when Herbert told me—about Mrs. Penray. Dying so sudden. I'd worked for her twenty years, such nice people, and it was a shock. A heart attack it was. I'd been back East visiting my daughter, I got home that Friday night, and when Herbert told me —well, I wanted to go and pay my respects at the grave. I felt bad about missing the funeral."

"So you took the bus, to come over to Forest Lawn, that Sunday."

"I don't know why you should want to hear all this, miss. Well, all right. Yes, I did. Herbert can't drive any more, since his sight went so bad. I got the Hollywood–Pasadena bus, the usual one I take to go to the Penrays', but I wasn't sure which city bus I had to transfer to."

"You got off at Broadway and Brand?"

"I suppose you've got some reason to be interested. That's right. I asked the bus driver and he wasn't sure either, he said I'd better ask a Glendale driver. I sat there and waited a long spell, and no buses came along at all. Finally a lady came and sat down on the bench, and I asked her, and she told me I ought to've stayed on the Hollywood bus up to Glendale Avenue. So I got the next Hollywood bus that came—"

"Have you any idea what time this was?" asked Delia.

"Well, as a matter of fact, I have," said Mrs. Penny. "Because I was feeling right annoyed at how slow these buses are, and only about one an hour, and I kept looking at my watch. I got the eleven-thirty bus at Vermont and Melrose, and it was about a quarter to twelve when I got off in Glendale, and I sat there for forty-five minutes waiting—longer. It was just about then when the lady told me I should have stayed on the bus, and there ought to be another one coming along, across the street. So I crossed over, and in about ten minutes another Hollywood bus came, and I got on it."

"Did anybody cross the street at the same time and get on the bus too?"

"Why, yes. I wouldn't recall, likely, if it hadn't been Sunday, but the streets were that empty, the buses too, and besides she got off when I did and walked down to the entrance to that place—Forest Lawn. Well, just a young girl—kind of light brown hair—I might recognize her again. It crossed my mind that she was going to visit a grave too, when she turned in there—she was walking a little ahead of me all the way down. But I don't know where she went. I hadn't realized that was such a big place, all those steep hills. I went into that office place to find out where Mrs. Penray's grave was, and the man just couldn't have been nicer. He said I couldn't walk up all that way, and he took me in a car—way up the hill it was—so I could leave my flowers on the grave."

And that, thought Delia in warm satisfaction, was very nice indeed.

Delia bought herself lunch at a Mannings coffee shop and drove back to Glendale.

Varallo and Forbes had just brought Guardino in; that had been a chase from one old address to another, a tedious piece of legwork. At Delia's gesture, Varallo let Forbes take him on to an interrogation room, and he and O'Connor listened to her triumphant results in silence.

"You can see for yourself, if Eileen was out of the house as early as that—it must have been the twelve-forty bus she got—she's in the clear. We knew she didn't do it anyway—" O'Connor asked how, and she told him.

"Hypnotists!" said O'Connor, scandalized. "My God! And who paid for his time, the city of Glendale? Or so you hope?"

"Don't nitpick. Marcella. But you can see—"

"Damn it, you're not paid to waste time kicking dead horses," said O'Connor. "Whether she did it or didn't, we're off the case. Forget it. So you're concerned, be concerned on your own time, for God's sake—if they charge her, you can hand all this rigmarole to her defense lawyer. Meanwhile, we've got enough on hand to work."

"Take it easy, Charles," said Varallo. "We've all been new and eager." He gave Delia a smile and went on down the hall.

Guardino said aggrievedly that it was a lousy world when being honest got you in trouble. He'd wanted to pay Carlos back, he was a nice guy, and the recorder had been part of his share of the loot. He'd never done no such thing before. But Roy, he took care of those peoples' yard and he said they went out practically every night, were gone a lot, and there was probably a lot of valuable stuff there. So they'd gone and busted in, and there was. Only they didn't know any real fences, they weren't real pros, and Roy had given the mink coat to his girlfriend and they were still trying to locate a fence for all the jewelry. Well, Roy Brown, he lived in Burbank.

"Doing what comes naturally," said Forbes. "So we go pick him up, and get the Goodmans in to identify all of it. She's going to have seven fits when she can't take it home with her.

———◆———

Fortunately, Delia had both a logical mind and a sense of humor; all O'Connor said was so, but it didn't stop her feeling annoyed. Everybody else was busy; O'Connor had gone down the hall after Varallo. The knit beret was still on his desk, and Delia picked it up. She thought, all right, damn it, so you're supposed to be working on a current case, not following up leads on a dead one; so go and do it.

Today's great thought, Varallo had said. Somebody might recognize it. And just how did you go about finding out? What it always came back to was the dogged legwork.

She took up the beret and went out again. It was nearly three o'clock and threatening rain. She drove down to that block on Adams, parked the Mercedes three doors down from the Jensen house, walked back to the corner, and started the canvass, door to door. The premise was logical. In a city this size, people weren't apt to be personally known to neighbors more than a block away. Other people, farther away, may have come in contact with Paul Jensen but not to be aware of where he lived, to hear any stray gossip about his having a houseful of cash.

In any case, work it. For three quarters of the block on this side there were all single houses. She hit every one. At two of them she got no answer. Everywhere else, a householder—mostly women—looked at the beret and didn't recognize it.

At four-fifty she came to an apartment building toward the corner of Green Street. Covering that took her to the end of her shift; there were twelve apartments, and someone at home in ten of them. Nobody had seen the knit beret before.

Delia called it a day and went home.

———◆———

There had been a third armed robbery overnight, but this time the bandit had picked the wrong man: a licensed private eye who was trained to notice things. He hadn't argued with the gun, but he could give them a good description and wanted to look at some mug shots. Katz took him downstairs after he'd made a statement.

Varallo and Forbes had picked up Roy Brown and the loot, and the Goodmans came in that morning to identify it formally. That delayed Delia from getting back to the legwork; she had to take another statement. As expected, Mrs. Goodman was indignant at having to leave everything at the police station. They trailed out finally, and Varallo said, "People," and offered Delia a cigarette.

Across the office, O'Connor slammed down the phone and said, "I told you so."

"What?"

"That was the DA's office. They don't want any part of it, thanks. Tied up in all the long words. In view of the husband's confession, and now suicide, and the very doubtful nature of the evidence, etc., etc., they don't feel it would be practical to bring a charge—waste the court's time, and so on, and so on. Which, God knows, is true. They'd never nail her. Any defense lawyer worth his down payment could make hay with all that."

"Not surprising, no," said Varallo. "Another case where we know who done it and our hands are tied. Or, if you're right," he added to Delia, "maybe we don't know and never will."

"Anyway, it's dead," said O'Connor.

Katz came in and said, "He made him. I'll bet it's the same boy on all three. Bernardo Blanco, he's got a little pedigree of B and E, shoplifting, couple of counts of public drunkenness, brawls. Anybody like to come help look for him? We haven't got a current address, it's a year and a half back."

"We have to start somewhere," said O'Connor, and got up.

Delia filed the Goodmans' statement and stretched wearily. It was getting on to lunchtime, it was going to start raining again any minute, and she didn't feel much like going out, but the job was out there on the street, at the legwork.

On the way she stopped for a hamburger at Bob's, and went back down to Adam. Just as she parked the Mercedes the first hesitant rain started to patter on the sidewalks. Resignedly she fished the plastic rainhood out of the glove compartment.

There was another apartment on the corner, with eighteen units. Fifteen of them had somebody home. Nobody had seen the beret before. Then a line of single houses, but seven of them had rental units in the rear, by time-honored California custom. Only one place didn't produce an answer to the doorbell. Nobody had seen the beret before. There was an apartment in the middle of the block. It was raining harder.

A big fat waste of time, thought Delia, coming out of that building at four-forty. Better admit it and go back to the office. Legwork, hah. But there were only four more single houses and then a smaller apartment. Nobody had ever said the job was fun, much less glamorous.

She plodded on. Half an hour later she came to the apartment— six units. At the ground-floor left, a gray old man said he'd never seen that thing before. At the ground-floor right, a plump blond woman with a can of beer in one hand looked at it and said, "Well, I will be— Where'd you find it? I swear to God, kids these days, don't know the value of a dollar and talk about careless! Sure I know it—it's my daughter Sheila's. I paid ten bucks for that thing at Webbs', for her birthday in November, and a month later she says she's lost it someplace, doesn't know where. As if money came off trees—where'd you find it, anyway?"

That turned out to be quite a session, and they all did some overtime. Delia called Varallo from the drugstore on the corner. "She says the girl's due home any minute. She's sixteen and never been in any trouble, a good girl."

"Before," said Varallo. "Charles will want to kiss you. We'll be right down."

Sheila Donovan had never been in any trouble: a rather plump, foolish-eyed teen-ager, hardly experienced with cops. When she came in and found them waiting for her, her mother just sitting looking shocked, O'Connor impatient, looking like a gangster at that end of the day, tall Varallo, she gave one look at the knit beret in Delia's hands and started to howl.

They got her to talk without much difficulty, through sobs. She told them the names right away. Her boyfriend Joe Ryan. His brother Dave.

"But the Ryans are nice people," said Mrs. Donovan numbly. "Oh, my God, I'll never understand why this had to happen—oh my God, your father'll be wild—"

Delia took them back to the station. Varallo and O'Connor brought the boys in fifteen minutes later, with an upset, blustering father. They explained all their rights. The boys were sixteen and fourteen, both good-sized for their ages. They'd never been in trouble either, and came apart without much prodding.

"We never meant to hurt him," said Joe, between sullenness and self-defense. "He was supposed to have a lot of money—ole miser—and Sheila and me, we thought make out like we were collecting for a camp fund or something, and she'd ask to go to the bathroom, see what she could pick up—but she said, take Dave along just in case. We never thought a real ole guy like that— But he was pretty big and strong, he was mad when we came right in, he grabbed me and he was shouting at us—everybody said he was crazy, ole miser, he was maybe going to *kill* us, and Dave got away from him, he just grabbed up that knife in the kitchen, he'd chased us out there—it was practically self-defense, the way he come at us, crazy ole guy—"

"We didn't know—he was dead—until everybody talking about it—" Sheila howling. "We were afraid he'd tell—he didn't, and we just thought because he was crazy—and there was only—there was only th-th-three dollars in his wallet!"

They had, of course, another session with the parents. It was ten-thirty before they got away from the station, and Rhys, sitting alone on night watch, had already been called out on a new homicide. But O'Connor was pleased with Delia; she was rather pleased with herself. She'd meant to stop and see Marcella and Eileen on her way home tonight, but that was the way the job sometimes went.

Delia got home at eleven-twenty and found both Alex and Steve waiting up for her over ham sandwiches. She had to tell them all about it, yawning; and Alex said fondly, "Haven't I always said it?

It's always the last little bit of the damned dull routine that pays off!"

――◆――

What with the new homicide—which turned out to be a knifing in a bar—another heist, and an attempted child molestation at Verdugo Park, Delia never got to California Street until after six on Saturday night. She had talked to Marcella yesterday, to tell them what the DA's office had decided.

Eileen was looking tired all over again, lying on the couch. "We had the funeral this morning," she said, not opening her eyes. "At that mortuary again, not even the church. But a lot of the church people came—the Dudeys and a lot of others. They meant to be kind. I think Mr. Dudey feels it's partly his fault, because he was the one who told Wesley about the church. I hope it wasn't."

"Well, it's over with," said Marcella. "It's all over with."

And eventually, thought Delia, unless the tax people grabbed it all on some technicality, Eileen ought to get at least a third of the old women's money, by California law. Unless she refused to take it, which was possible—the way she was still talking.

"No, it isn't over with," she was saying without any emphasis. "It'll never be all over until I've paid for it somehow. So they aren't going to arrest me. Well, I'll have to pay for it some other way."

"My dear child, we've told you—when Dr. Wagner had you under, you told us exactly what happened, and you didn't have anything to do with killing her! You said you just threw the scissors at her and ran out—"

"And," said Delia, "it was too early. Because I've found your nice colored woman, and she remembered what time it was."

"Who?"

"You told us about her," said Delia, and told them about Mrs. Rachel Penny. "You must have gotten that bus at about twelve-forty, Eileen. About fifteen minutes after Wesley left the house. You were up at Broadway and Brand by ten minutes to one. And Mrs. Endicott was stabbed between one and two."

But Eileen was shaking her head. "All of that doesn't matter," she said quietly. "I heard you say, before, that the doctor said he couldn't be exactly sure what time she was killed. And really, there wasn't anybody but me who hated her enough to kill her. All right, if I was on that bus then, and up at Forest Lawn, I'd killed her before I went out. I must have."

"Because of that damned dream?" Marcella was exasperated.

"Yes, because of the Dream. Coming true at last. All the years I've had it, there was always that terrible knowledge that I'd done something—something so bad, so wrong—and I wouldn't have felt like that, don't you see, if I hadn't. And then it really happened—after all those years—and I had the same feeling. So *I know*," said Eileen.

Marcella shut her mouth hard. "The doom assigned."

"If you want to call it that."

"That dream—" said Delia. Marcella looked at her hopefully, as if she could convince Eileen with just a couple of official words. "What was your maiden name?"

"Why? Oh, Burke. Eileen Mary Burke."

"Do you have a birth certificate? Were you born in Sacramento?"

"I don't know, I suppose so. I never had to have one."

"What's on your mind?" asked Marcella curiously.

"I don't quite know. I'd better not say in case it fizzles out," said Delia. And she thought, no use going up over Sunday.

Another thing Alex always had taught her was to follow through and clear up all the loose ends.

———◆———

Delia came in early on Monday morning and said to O'Connor composedly, "I hope you don't mind, Lieutenant—I'm taking a couple of days off. If I get back Tuesday I'll come in Wednesday instead, so that'll only make one day. But I am allowed six days' sick leave a year and I'm never sick, so I'll make it up." And just what she thought she might accomplish in two days—

"Where the hell do you think you're going, after three months on the job?"

"Finishing up a case," said Delia. "Can't I take a day after breaking Jensen for you?"

"Breaking cases is your job," said O'Connor; but his mouth quirked into a grin. "Where the hell are you going?"

"Hunting," said Delia, "for a dream. Because there is such a thing as free will, and I don't believe in assigned doom."

———◆———

On the flight to Sacramento, she wondered, where exactly does memory begin? Four, five, six? The rest silence, maybe before the conscious mind was fully developed. And she was proceeding blind; she didn't know any dates, how many foster homes (probably impossible to trace down now), where, what, why.

But one thing she did know: If the twentieth century had a mania, it was for collecting and filing records; especially anything any part of government administered, there would be voluminous records.

The plane landed at ten-thirty. She rented a car at the airport, bought a city map—she'd never been there before—checked into a motel, and managed to find the central offices of the city welfare services, the office of Aid to Dependent Children. The badge, of course, was very helpful. Finally she met a Mrs. Talmadge, probably a fixture there for years, gray-haired and inured to the bureaucracy, who got interested.

"You don't know how long ago?"

"Anything up to twenty-two years."

"Goodness. All the records that old will be on microfilm. So many children—it's a sad place to work in, in a way, Miss Riordan. Even on paper, just in the office. Never enough foster homes, never enough good ones. The children are the innocent victims. I can open all the records to you and explain how they're filed, but you'll have to do the looking, we're always busy."

"That's fine," said Delia. And that was at three o'clock.

She learned after a while to take just one quick glance, through the viewer, at the name; presently she was running the film through faster. But when the office closed at six she still hadn't found Eileen Mary Burke, and she was up to 1960. She took herself out to dinner and went back to the motel; she'd brought plenty to read.

At eight on Tuesday morning she was back at the viewer. And at nine-ten she found the name. Eileen Mary Burke, handed over to the agency as an orphan at the age of five and a half, in 1962. And not Sacramento: a place called Deer Grove. An address given, the orphan's home until she was handed over. Bright Avenue. She copied all the data and consulted Mrs. Talmadge.

"Oh yes. Outlying suburb," said Mrs. Talmadge at once. "We'd be the nearest agency."

"Well," said Delia, having looked it up on the map, "I may as well start there, but I may want to come back and follow up the case, find the various foster homes, talk to—"

"Impossible," said Mrs. Talmadge wearily. "Most of them would be gone with the wind after all this time. You could try, I suppose. If I knew what you were looking for—"

"I wish I knew myself," said Delia.

She drove out of the city a little way to Deer Grove. It might have grown in sixteen years; it still wasn't very big, something like three thousand population. She stopped at a service station and was directed to Bright Avenue. It was a short, narrow street of single houses, none of them very big or new. The address she'd copied down was a little white frame house with a picket fence in front. There were children in the yard, and a dog.

It didn't look like a town where people moved frequently, or far.

Delia parked and went up to the house on the right next to that one. The woman who opened the door was about sixty, short and stout, pleasant-faced, gray-haired. Delia showed her the badge and she looked concerned, interested. "What is it?"

"I'm looking for someone who might know something about the Burkes, who used to live next door. There was a little girl—"

"Eileen," said the woman. "Well, after all these years! If that's not the funniest thing— I was thinking of them just the other day. Yes, we lived here then. I'm Mrs. Holst—Mrs. Norman Holst. Step in. Why on earth should a policewoman be asking about the Burkes, and them dead and gone all these years?"

"It's nothing to do with the police," said Delia. "I'm a friend of Eileen's. She's never known anything about her parents, her background, and as I was coming up here I said I'd look. My name's Riordan."

"Well, if that isn't a queer thing, Miss Riordan. My thinking of them just the other day, and you turning up like this. I'd be real interested to hear about Eileen, doesn't seem possible she'll be twenty-one, twenty-two, now. Well, I can tell you a bit. They came here from the city, he had a job at an insurance agency here. Bob Burke, his name was, and she was Maureen. Nice young people." She'd got Delia settled in a chair in a fussy prim living room where doilies decorated all the furniture. "Oh, that was a real tragedy, Miss Riordan. A real tragedy. Like the minister says, in the midst of life."

"What happened?"

"Why, he had this awful cancer. One minute a big strong young fellow in the prime of life—he was only thirty-two—and six months later he's in his grave. And as if that wasn't bad enough, then she was taken too." A big black-and-white cat came into the room and leaped onto Mrs. Holst's lap, and she stroked it automatically. "It was like fate didn't mean them to be apart, but the poor child—"

"What happened to Mrs. Burke?"

"Killed!" said Mrs. Holst dramatically. "Killed in an instant, along with poor Mr. Truax, right in the middle of the main street across from the bank. It was right here in this very room I heard about it, from Frank Allison. The fire chief. And Eileen was right here too." She drew a half-pleasurable breath, remembering shock and horror and drama. "You see, after her husband died, they gave her a job at the insurance agency. And Eileen was in kindergarten then, up to noon, and Mrs. Burke asked if I'd look after her, in the afternoons, till she got home. She paid me, of course. It wasn't much trouble, me having raised three of my own already then—but that little thing," she laughed, "quick as lightning she was, you had to keep an eye on her. And watch out she didn't get hold of matches—seemed like she was fascinated with lighted matches. Her mother was always after her about it. Why, not long before it happened she'd come to pick her up one afternoon and Eileen set a whole book of matches alight, and Mrs. Burke told her if she ever played with matches again she'd go away and leave her and never come back, and a policeman would come for her. Not that I think it's such a good idea to make children scared of police, but there, we've all got our own ways with children."

"How was she killed?"

"Oh, it was terrible! She and Mr. Truax had just come out of the insurance office, they were crossing the street to the little restaurant there for lunch—Maggie Crawford had it then, her daughter's running it now—when this car came down the street about eighty miles an hour and ran right over them! They found out later the driver was drunk, he was some fellow from the city—he crashed the car in a ditch outside town and he got hurt too but not too bad—the drunks never do. The fire station's just down the street, and Frank Allison was the first one got to them, he saw it all. And he knew I looked after the little girl, he came to tell me." Another long breath. "He sat right there in that chair you're sitting in, and, 'Mrs. Holst,' he said, 'it was deliberate murder. It was deliberate murder,' he said, and he was right." She was pleased with the rapt way Delia was listening.

"Was he wearing his uniform?" asked Delia.

"What? Why, yes, he was. And I said I surely hoped they'd catch the man who did it—that was before we knew he'd crashed the car—and he told me we'd have to leave that to the police detectives. 'I don't know why it had to happen!' I told him, and he said God must have some reason, and anyway, we couldn't do anything for her now. Or poor Mr. Truax—he left a wife and three children. But poor little Eileen—neither of the Burkes had any family, and it was a real tragedy for her. And bless me, just as we were sitting here talking about it I happened to turn around and there the child was, with a paper book of matches in her hand too. Thank God, I thought, she was too young to take it all in."

Delia had been listening, fascinated. "I suppose," she said, "you had a cat then, too."

Thrown off stride, Mrs. Holst said, "What? Well, I usually have a cat—I like a cat around the place. Let's see, that'd be sixteen and a half years ago, I guess I still had old Molly, she was a silver tabby. One thing I'll say for Eileen, for such a little thing she was real gentle with the cat, real good. It went to my heart to see that social welfare lady take her away, after they'd found there weren't any relatives, but there wasn't anything I could do. Mrs. Burke was only paying on the house, she just had her salary. I'd have liked to have taken the child, but it'd have been too much. My husband wasn't well, and my oldest girl's husband was out of work then, we had to help them." She regarded Delia, bright-eyed with interest. "I'd be real interested, hear how Eileen turned out. She was a nice little girl. I'm sorry I couldn't tell you more about the Burkes, who their people were, but all I knew of them, they were nice, good people."

Delia drew a long breath. "Well, you've told me quite a lot."

Eileen looked at her rather wildly. "You mean it wasn't *waiting*—it had already *happened?*"

"I didn't like that dream, you know," said Delia. She took Marcella's proffered cigarette. "Do you know the first thing I didn't like about it? The brass buttons. Policemen don't have brass buttons now, not for a long time. And it wasn't likely that a policeman would use the word 'murder' to a civilian. And the other things that were said in the dream were quite ordinary."

"But they frightened me so! I know there wasn't any logical reason they should, but they did! And it was always then I knew I'd done something—just terrible, whatever had happened was all my fault, I could never be punished enough—"

"Maybe you were punished enough," said Delia gravely. "You see, according to Mrs. Holst, your mother had told you that if you ever played with matches again she'd go away and leave you. And you did. And you never saw her again—she went away. And what you thought was a policeman came. And you were taken away. It all fitted in, to your six-year-old mind. And every once in a while it would come back as a nightmare, and I'm not surprised."

"I will be damned," said Marcella to herself. "But it fits, all right."

"Like time," said Eileen wonderingly. "Running backward and forward. If we knew about it. The Dunne man. But if that's all it was—all it ever was—" She drew a long, long breath. "It didn't really mean anything at all—and there never was any—any doom."

"I don't think there's ever any certain doom," said Delia, and Marcella's eyes met hers warmly.

---◆►---

They had picked up Bernardo Blanco, and the private eye had identified him. The juvenile killers had been released to the parents' custody on bail; a court hearing was scheduled. Considering their ages, they'd probably be put on probation until they were adults.

There were three new heists and another burglary. And the official word had come through, Katz's appointment as sergeant.

Busy as they were, Varallo and O'Connor were interested in what O'Connor called her side trip. But they were, she had found, good detectives, and good detectives were always interested in people, what made them tick.

Eileen would be all right. With Marcella—or even on her own—she would be all right.

---◆►---

On Saturday afternoon at about three o'clock, Patrolman Stoner was idly cruising down a side street toward Central when he spotted a kid breaking a rear window in a house and starting to climb inside. He curbed the car, reported in, and went to collar the kid. It was a little frame house behind a church on the corner, and it didn't look as if it would contain much valuable.

When he brought the kid in, he reported all that and left him to the detectives. As far as Stoner was concerned, the detectives could have all the brainwork and paperwork. They might make more money, but they also ran the risk of ulcers and high blood pressure.

The detectives who were in—Delia, Varallo, and O'Connor—looked at the kid. He was Stanley Clifford. He was shaking all over, scared out of his mind. He looked back at them and said, "I wasn't going to steal anything! Just—just get something back. That's all."

"What?" asked Delia.

"A book. That's all, a book. It didn't belong to him," said Stanley.

"Who?"

"Him. The pastor. He said it was a dirty book—I guess it is—but it wasn't his! It wasn't mine either, it belongs to Tom Linker, this guy I know at school—he bought it, he paid five bucks for it, and he wants it back! I hafta keep telling him I forgot— I *asked* the pastor, I mean I *told* him, but he wouldn't pay me no mind—"

Varallo looked at Delia with raised brows. Her mind made a little jump, and she said, "That was about a month ago, wasn't it, that he took the dirty book away from you?"

"I guess. Yeah." He was sweating.

"And wouldn't give it back. Did you ever have some idea before today of getting in to take it back?"

Stanley looked at her as fearfully as if she were a witch. "I—I never broke in a window there before. I didn't."

"Did you have that idea?" asked Varallo.

"He didn't have no right to it—it wasn't his! But he wouldn't listen—and Tom kept saying, 'Give it back or pay me five bucks—' And now, Mom says after the pastor died his wife moved, I thought the house was empty and I could get in and might find it— I never got a chance to look when I was in there that day—" He shut up and went pasty white under the red acne scars.

"When you were in there that Sunday?" asked O'Connor in a hard voice. "And found the old lady home alone?"

"Oh, Jesus, oh, God," said Stanley. "I never meant nothing like that! I never meant it! I—I had to get that book back, he hadn't no right to keep it! I—after we got home from church, I told Mom I was going out to get a hamburger, and I sort of hung around the hamburger place a while and then I went back to the church—and—there wasn't any car in the garage, I'd never been behind the church before to see that house, I just knew he lived there—the pastor—and I thought, everybody gone somewhere in the car—I—the front door was unlocked and I just went in—"

The old woman in her wheelchair in the living room, probably still furious at Eileen.

"I just went in—and she was there—that old lady—she was shouting at me and she had some scissors in her hand—I—Mom'd be so mad, and I was scared—I just—" He was rabbit with snake, facing them terrified. "I didn't mean to do it! I did it before I knew I was doing it—those scissors—"

After a moment Varallo said gently, "So at last we know."

They got to the routine. He was a juvenile; they notified the mother. Told them about rights. Applied for the warrant. Booked him in. So it was out of their hands, up to the DA's office, where it would get called voluntary, involuntary manslaughter, with or without detention. Probation for certain.

"It had to be that kind of thing," said Varallo. "The irrationality —the moment's panic impulse."

"And just a one-in-a-million chance we ever dropped on him," said O'Connor. "Once in a while we get the breaks. Fate smiling on us for a change." It was ten after six. "Let's call it a day and go home. Saturday night again. What do you want to bet, a couple of new heists overnight?"

It had, after the rain and the subsequent cold, turned a lot warmer again, nice and sunny, up to seventy-five today. Pulling into the drive of the house on Hillcroft Road, to Laura and the children, and Gideon Algernon Cadwallader playing watchcat, Varallo thought about his roses. Damn it, they needed all the sun they could get. So unwrap all the burlap. And, February now being advanced, then have another cold snap and the threat of freezing. You really couldn't win.

O'Connor shut the driveway gate and braced himself. Maisie plunged at him frantically. They went into the kitchen together.

"You're late," said Katharine. "Just listen to the silence, Charles. Isn't it wonderful? He's being an angel. Just, belatedly, like that obnoxiously angelic one of Laura's. Good day, darling?"

"Let's say, something accomplished, something done," said O'Connor. He shed jacket, tie, and shoulder holster on the living-room couch, and fixed before-dinner drinks. They took the drinks down to the nursery, and he surveyed Vincent Charles, dreamily smiling up at them, with approval. "Now that he's starting to get civilized, Katy, I guess I can start to appreciate having an offspring. And by the way, our female detective's coming on all right. She's a good girl."

———————◆———————

Delia came in the back door and sniffed. It was Alex's special, rich beef stew with biscuits on top, a spinach soufflé, and tomato aspic salad. She went down the hall. They were in the middle of a chess game, both bent intently over the board between wheelchair and couch.

They were going to be interested to hear about Stanley Clifford.